Azathoth Rising

A History of *The Necronomicon*

Joseph S. Dale

Strategic Book Publishing and Rights Co.

Copyright © 2016 Joseph S. Dale. All rights reserved.

No part of this book may be reproduced or transmitted in any form or by any means, graphic, electronic, or mechanical, including photocopying, recording, taping, or by any information storage retrieval system, without the permission, in writing, of the publisher. For more information, send an email to support@sbpra.net, Attention Subsidiary Rights Department.

Strategic Book Publishing and Rights Co., LLC
USA | Singapore
www.sbpra.com

For information about special discounts for bulk purchases, please contact Strategic Book Publishing and Rights Co., LLC Special Sales, at bookorder@sbpra.net.

ISBN: 978-1-68181-327-1

Dedicated to Con, who introduced me to the world of H. P. Lovecraft and is the best friend a man could ever want. Thanks, pal.

Profound thanks to the late, great H. P. Lovecraft for the use of his Cthulhu Mythos, upon which this story is loosely based.

I have used considerable literary license in this story, which I hope the purist reader will forgive. Other than actual historical figures, no character in this story is meant to represent any person, living or dead. Such an occurrence is purely coincidencental.

"This is the Book of the Black Earth—The Book of Dead Names—that I have set down in peril of my life …"

                                              Prelude to *The Necronomicon*
                                                       Abdul Al-Hazred

Chapter One

AD 645
Damascus

* * *

Several miles to the south of the great city of Damascus, to the side of the As-Suwayda Road, stood an old, decrepit stone and thatch hut. To look at it, one would think it was abandoned—derelict, but such was not the case.

* * *

The old Arab sat at the rough wooden table, his head in his hands. It was almost finished. All those days and weeks and months of writing, but he must work faster. The voices in his head were getting louder, almost by the hour—especially that old one, the one known to him, the one that would soon become known to many as Azathoth. He must get all the chants and spells down so that the powers of the "Old Ones" could be countered.

Abdul Al-Hazred had studied mysticism, magic and metaphysics since he was a young man, questioning those throughout the lands of Palestine, Syria, Polemon and Cappadocia. He had travelled far and wide through the old Kingdom of Babylon, even making a special three-year trip to the ancient City of Ur in Chaldea, to consult the wise men there. One man who had helped him more than any other—one of the priests from Sumer—was a man named Nephren-Ka. The two had gone over many spells and Nephren-Ka had looked carefully at each one, changing a word here and a pronunciation there, to get each one, he said, exactly right.

Al-Hazred looked hard at the spells, seeing few differences in the two versions. Finally, at Nephren-Ka's insistence, he chose the updated versions and committed them to memory—a colossal enterprise for one so old. Although he did manage it, he refused to use the chants, for he considered himself too old to undertake such responsibility. At sixty-three, he was considered extremely old in those days, when the average age of death for a man was thirty-four. So he had taken his many memories of the great spells and chants and, with great courage, begun a single scroll containing them all, together with descriptions of how each could be used, as well as considerable philosophies he had discovered. He thought long and hard over a title for the book and one evening while listening to the night sounds, he came across it. The sounds of the night were, as he well knew, made by little insects of the night, but long before his lifetime, others—more primitive—believed the noises were caused by evil demons called *Al Azif* (Demon Song) in the old Aramaic tongue. With a slight smile, Al-Hazred realized that here was his title. He quickly turned to the first page and wrote across the top:

In Arabic it means Demon Song. In English it translates as Names of the Dead and in Latin it is *The Necronomicon*.

All right, he had a title, so now he must finish his book as quickly as possible. As soon as it was well under way, Nephren-Ka took his leave. Al-Hazred was sorry to see his friend go, but he thought all men must follow their destinies. So he bid farewell to the man and returned to the task. Now that he was on the verge of completing *Al Azif*, he thought about the wording and the lovely poetry of the various parts. Some detached part of his mind noted wryly that he had used almost fifty reed quills to write it and realizing this helped to take his mind off the terrors of what could happen. Knowing he must go on—in spite of the fear and despair threatening to overwhelm him—he turned once again to the page and wrote feverishly.

* * *

Meanwhile, two travellers, Akbar and Fadil, were walking along the desert road on their way to worship at the mosque in Damascus. They approached the hut, casting fearful glances at the gathering storm clouds above. They did not want to spend the night in the desert, especially with the storm brewing and the threat of a possible downpour.

"Allah's blessings be upon this house," called Fadil, in the time-honored manner, as they pushed aside the beaded curtain and entered the first empty room. There was no reply. They became aware of a scratching, rather like a mouse eating. Realising it was somebody writing they passed through the inner door and came upon the old Arab. Without even an upward glance, he waved them to a wooden bench and continued writing. Glancing at each other, the two men took their seats, aware that they would not get any more out of this strange person until he finished his work.

Suddenly the old Arab groaned. "Ah … the shadows. They're closing in."

Realising something was wrong the two men swallowed hard and looked at each other. Akbar stood, intending to offer assistance but was waved down again.

Al-Hazred was almost finished—just the final sentence and his lineage were left. *Amen!* His pen swept out the wide, detailed Arabic characters, *I have completed it. Naught more can I do. The future is in thy hands, thou who shall read this writing.* He dipped his pen and began writing his name and lineage.

"This is the book of the servant of the gods … ." And that was as far as he got.

Thunder crashed across the sky, but it was as nothing compared to the roar of triumph that resounded and echoed inside his head. In his terror, he leaped from his chair, scattering the pens and inkpot all over the floor. It was happening. In the last vestige of his sanity, Al-Hazred realised that he had done all in his power to counter the evil of the nameless ones.

Sheer terror struck his heart. "Oh, my god and goddess," he screamed, "save me from the powers of the Old Ones and the horrors of beyond."

A voice roared with evil laughter.

"Thy god and goddess will not help thee now!" *it bellowed.* ***"I, Azathoth, the Crawling Chaos, have won! Be aware, mortal and despair. The spells and chants that thou hast so carefully writ, far from binding, will release. Nyarlathotep, my servant, who has changed the wording of the chants and thus has he changed their meanings. If any of thy kind should say them, they will turn the key of the door to the outer circles and once opened, it can never be closed. The old gods will be released. Thou hast doomed the whole of thy pitiful human race to destruction!"***

The voice roared with laughter and with a scream of despair, the old Arab reached out to the manuscript in a desperate attempt to destroy that which he had written, but it was far too late. Al-Hazred's aged heart failed him and he collapsed. He was dead before he hit the earthen floor.

Akbar and Fadil sat terrified, staring at the still figure, while the storm overhead roared in its ferocity. There was no movement as lightning lit up the room in a startling series of flashes. Thunder roared almost continuously as the rain pelted down. Eventually the crashes of thunder diminished into fragmentary mutters on the horizon. When the rain slackened to a light drizzle and eventually ceased, the men hesitantly went to the body. Akbar nudged it with a toe. There was no response.

"He's ... dead."

The two men paused while they gathered their courage. Then Fadil went to the table.

"We'll never know who he was," he said, indicating the last unfinished page which was now marked with a long pen line.

"Perhaps it's just as well," replied the other with a shudder, remembering the last terror-filled words of the man.

They gathered the pile of parchment together and delivered it to the Vizier of the Caliph of Damascus, Wakil Ben Abdul, well known for his wisdom.

"Do you know who he was?" asked the wise man.

The two shook their heads. "Nay," replied Akbar. "All we know is that he was writing in a small hovel several leagues to the south of Damascus to the side of the As-Suwayda Road."

The Vizier nodded. "I see. There is only one man who lived there—a madman named Abdul Al-Hazred. At least," he corrected himself, "many thought him to be mad."

"He died before our eyes during a thunderstorm. His last words were 'Oh, my god and goddess, save me from the powers of the Old Ones and the horrors of beyond.'"

Ben Abdul sighed. "I see. Well I'm afraid that he is very probably beyond human help now, or indeed any help. Is his body nearby?"

The men nodded and led him outside where the body of the old Arab was lying on a stretcher prior to burial.

"Yes," nodded Ben Abdul sadly, "that's Al-Hazred all right. May Allah have mercy on his soul."

They all nodded sadly.

An hour or so later the two men buried the body in the sand outside the city and offered up prayers for his soul. But all were despairingly of the opinion that it was far too late for that.

Wakil Ben Abdul had made scrolls from sheets before and glued the pile of parchment together with great care into a full scroll. As he did so, he read the various pages. The more he read the more something in the back of his mind warned him against trying the spells, tempted though he was to do so. A chill went down his spine and he swallowed hard. There was something about this scroll which was unwholesome: evil. He rolled the completed scroll up, tying it with three leather thongs and placed it in his retreat library some miles to the southeast in the middle of the desert. As far as they were all concerned, it was the end of the matter, but it was a long time before any of them could sleep a full night.

And there, in the depths of the wise man's library, waiting to be discovered, lay *Al Azif: The Necronomicon*.

Chapter Two

AD 657
Quatana, the Syrian Desert

Rafi was very unhappy with his lot. The young boy climbed up the library ladder to the top and began to search wearily for the scroll that his master, Wakil Ben Abdul, had ordered him to find.

Rafi was the son of Faruq, an elderly potter, who wanted something better for his boy, as all fathers did. So, after giving him a perfunctory education in reading and counting, Faruq took Rafi to Damascus, to study under the Vizier, Wakil Ben Abdul, whose fame as a wise man was widely known, but as the days passed, it seemed to Rafi that all Wakil wanted was a slave. Rafi was required to tidy up after Wakil, serve him his food, pour him his wine and while the wise man was in Damascus—sometimes for days at a time—clean the retreat. The sum total of his learning was exactly zero.

Rafi thought on these things and felt badly let down as he continued looking for the book. Then a parchment scroll caught his eye. It was loosely bound with three leather thongs and looked quite dirty. But something made Rafi unfasten the thongs and unroll it. The Arabic title sprawled across the top of the first page and Rafi began to pick out the words: *Demon Song—The Book of Dead Names*. Rafi's eyebrows raised in curiosity. He seated himself on the ladder and began to read in earnest.

An hour later when he heard Wakil approaching, he quickly rolled up and replaced the scroll on the shelf, then made a show of searching. Wakil came through the curtain and upbraided the boy roundly for wasting his time. Rafi bore the uproar stoically and when it was finished, he went on with his work. But in his head he was remembering the few pages he had read and how much power the scroll must contain.

That night, Rafi listened for Wakil's guttural snore and when it came he crept from his pallet, slipped into the library and took the book down from the shelf. Then, taking three rushlights he quickly made his way out into the desert. There was a circle of rocks called standing stones—made by some long dead pagan civilization as a sacred site—near an outcrop about fifty meters to the north. Rafi made his way to the centre, lit a rushlight and settled himself comfortably.

Untying the thongs, he unrolled the book on the sand, found the page he had left and began again. It must have been an eerie sight; a boy sitting by himself in the middle of an ancient circle of rocks, reading an old tome. Twice he had to return to the house to get more rushlights, but after seven hours solid he finally finished. *What a book and what power it could wield*, he thought. There were many spells: one granted visions while in sleep; another conjured up what it described as "the globes of knowledge," and still another banished all enemies from around the caster.

Several times, Rafi found himself unconsciously mouthing the tongue-twisting words which made up the spells. Although they were written in Arabic the words were actually ancient Sumerian— what could best be described as Arabic-phonetic and totally unknown to his tongue. When he saw the unfinished sentence on the last page and the streak of ink across it he shuddered. He re-rolled to the various pages, stopping finally on one and he knew what he could do. The words stared up at him: Opening Door of Power, Knowledge and Enlightenment. Wakil would no longer be his master. Rafi would teach the man a thing or two.

Suddenly he became aware of a gathering light. Looking up he realized in surprise that the sun was almost ready to rise. In a slight panic, he rose, dusted the sand from his body, rolled the book together, retied the thongs and quickly returned it to the library. Then, as if he had just spent the whole night asleep, he prepared Wakil's breakfast.

That day was a long one for Rafi, but he was able to steal several seemingly unrelated items: a small square of copper plate, a silk handkerchief, a reed pen and some ink and a pure beeswax candle. He hid these items under his pallet and waited for sunset, but the boy was so tired that sleep overtook him before he could put his plan into practice. He woke just as the sun was ready to rise, cursed himself as a sluggard and began the day as normal. At least he felt refreshed.

The day went very slowly for the boy but finally the sun dipped toward the horizon. When Wakil dowsed the rush lamps, Rafi lay in bed waiting for Wakil's guttural snore to tell him that his master was asleep and then he quickly slid out of bed. Reclaiming the book and his pack of items, he made his way to the circle of rocks and lit a rushlight. The spell had to be cast in a very wide open place and the desert was ideal for that.

Following the instructions, Rafi began to write several strange figures in ink on the copper square. When he finished, he wrapped it in the silk. One of the huge stones had fallen on its side and it was an obvious altar. He laid the silk package in the middle and then broke the beeswax candle in two. Lighting each half, he set them at each end of the makeshift altar.

With preparations complete, it was now time for the spell. Heart pounding and sweat beading his brow Rafi carefully unrolled the book to the chant for opening the door. The book stated that the door needed to be open for the power to become available. Rafi swallowed hard and began to read aloud, haltingly at first, but then with increasing confidence, as his mouth grew used to the words.

Meanwhile, Wakil was restless. His mind was producing nightmare after nightmare. Finally, he sat bolt upright, with the memory of a horrifying monster about to rip him in two. He breathed a deep sigh of relief as the monster collapsed into the familiar and comforting surroundings of his home. *Oh, thank Allah. Only a dream.* Wiping his face of sweat, Wakil sat there as his heart steadied and after a second or two, rose and went in search of a drink. The wine amphora was still half-full and after taking a small draught to sweeten his mouth, Wakil walked back toward his bed. On the way he had to pass near Rafi's place. He looked over at the pallet and saw it was empty. *He has possibly gone to answer a call of nature*, thought Wakil, but something made the man stop. It was not normal for Rafi to be taken short at that time. He was only a young lad and it was only the second watch of the night. Rafi should still be sleeping soundly.

Feeling just slightly silly, but also a little worried, Wakil walked out onto the sand. He had built this place far away from cities years ago, so his studying would not be disturbed. He divided his time between this retreat and Damascus as Vizier to the great Caliph.

The desert was dark and silent and overhead the universe was shining brilliantly. Then, just as Wakil was shaking his head at what he saw as needless worry, he saw the small light shining in the near distance somewhere by the circle of rocks. Remembering Rafi, Wakil swallowed at the thought of bandits. The boy could be in danger. Drawing his robe around him, Wakil hurried toward the light.

Rafi was sweating hard. He had just realised that he was no longer saying the words; they were saying themselves. The boy stood there with the unknown words pouring from his lips. They finally came to an end and were replaced by deathly silence all around. Even the breeze was stilled. There was a pause and Rafi's heart seemed to stop beating. Sweat poured down his face and his mind went blank with fear as he waited.

Then, just as he was beginning to think that nothing would

happen and was about to relax, a voice spoke inside his head, yet seemed to echo everywhere, like the Imam's call to prayer from the top of the temple.

"Thou has called me and I have come. What wouldst thou with me?"

Rafi's mouth dropped open in terror. He was shivering so much that he could hardly speak. His heart felt ready to burst from his chest. "Wh … who are you?" he finally blurted.

"I am known as Azathoth. Thou must say my name to open the door to knowledge and power. Draw near. Behold, I have set the path before thee."

A silver pathway appeared leading to the mightiest double door that Rafi had ever seen. The door was even bigger than the Great Gate of Damascus he had seen several years before. Gathering what little courage remained, Rafi set his foot on the path and began to walk toward the door and thought of the power which would be his when the door opened.

Then suddenly there came a well-known voice. "Rafi. In Allah's name, what do you think you are doing?" It was Wakil, but Rafi no longer feared this man.

"Wakil Ben Abdul. I will no longer be your slave," he cried defiantly. "Now I will have the power to be whoever I want to be. I will be the ruler of all. I shall know all things and you cannot stop me."

Wakil stopped dead. "What have you done? What power are you talking about?"

"The power from beyond," Rafi replied smugly, "the power you had but did not use."

"What are you talking about?" Wakil repeated in fear. "What power?"

"It was from a scroll in your library."

Wakil swallowed. There were many dangerous books in his library. His heart almost seemed to stop beating and his teeth clenched in horrified anticipation. "What? Which book is that?"

"The Book of Dead Names—*Al Azif*."

The man's face went dead white under his swarthiness. "*Al Azif*? Oh no. It is the book of all lies."

For the first time, Rafi felt the stirrings of doubt. "What do you mean, lies? How do you know?"

"I have studied it and there are many parts which are not as they say. In fact, they are evil. Which spell did you attempt to cast?"

Rafi's mouth opened and shut in confusion. Finally, he pulled himself together. "It was described as Opening the Door to All Power, Knowledge and Enlightenment.

Wakil's jaw clenched tightly. "Oh no, not that." he muttered, then cried out, "You must have had contact with the nether world. Who have you spoken to?"

Rafi hesitated. "I don't know. It said its name was Az … something."

"*Aahh*." shrieked Wakil in sudden terror. "Don't say it. Whatever you do, don't—say—that—name. I know the entity. It is evil. In the name of Allah and your own immortal soul, come away. You must, or the doors to The pit will be opened."

Then suddenly a voice roared in both their minds.

"*Wakil Ben Abdul. I know thee. Thou wouldst not open the door before and refused to let anyone else in. Now thou shalt watch as thine apprentice opens the door and is damned for eternity. And,*" the voice finished smugly, "*there is nothing that thou canst do about it.*"

When the voice of Azathoth roared out its horrible message, Rafi realised that Wakil was right. At the bottom of his soul, he knew perfectly well that Wakil was not nearly as bad as he had painted him. As silence fell, Rafi made up his mind and turned to Wakil.

"Master," he cried, "forgive me. What can be done?"

"Come to me quickly," shouted Wakil, holding out his arms. Rafi tried to move, but he felt like he was trying to run through quicksand. The boy felt a chill slide all the way down his spine. Oh no, what was to happen now. He had through his ignorance destroyed his eternal soul.

Azathoth's roar of victory resounded through his head and Rafi could hardly think. Each foot seemed to weigh a ton. The boy felt his body begin to collapse under the sheer weight of Azathoth's power. He was being dragged ever nearer to the terrible door, which up until a few moments ago he would have walked toward gladly. With all the power in his young body, he tried to run, but all his strength seemed to have disappeared. He was doomed. The boy gave a long shriek of terrified despair. Nothing could save him now.

Then came Wakil's voice, clear and calm, as he recited the creed of Islam, the only Power of Good that he knew. "Listen, you monster. 'There is no God but Allah and Mohammad is the prophet, the prophet of Allah. I call upon Allah the all powerful, the almighty.'" He paused and something prompted him to add. "And all powers of good in the universe now, to break your power. Rafi, move!"

Azathoth gave an ear-splitting roar of frustration as his power faded against the irresistible Power of Good. Rafi heard the confidence in his master's voice and the man's final order gave him the impetus he needed. With a super-human effort, using strength he did not know he had, he managed to break away from the power of the Dark One and race to his master. The boy cannoned into the man, his arms grasping around the man's middle so hard he almost crushed him. In spite of the horror of the situation, Wakil gave a wry grin and clasped the boy's body to him.

Azathoth continued to roar in frustration and Wakil bit his lip hard. He could feel the monster drawing in its power for a final terrible assault. He drew Rafi close. The old man's mouth was dry and his eyes grew wide. If the monster released his power, it would be all over for Rafi and Wakil and for Earth as well. This power would herald a new and terrible age of darkness, terror and horror.

Gritting his teeth, Wakil made up his mind. He never thought he would ever be called on to take such drastic, extreme measures. His heart was racing in terror as he flung an arm in the air, drew a strange figure in midair and took in a breath as if to shout. Then in a clear, ringing voice he pronounced the last two lines of the deadly Sussama ritual, *"Which must not be done unless the soul itself is in deathly peril."*

There was a short pause and Wakil had the impression the monster could not believe what had been done, but it worked. A white light, blinding in its intensity, flooded the whole area. The voice of Azathoth screamed in agony and frustration, then sank swiftly into silence and the great door and path disappeared into the darkness.

For a moment there was a deathly quiet. Rafi still clung to his master, trembling in aftershock, his eyes closed tight waiting, so to speak, for the axe to fall. When he opened them and looked up at Wakil, the man was looking ahead. The light had coalesced into a cool, brilliantly shining circle and from it came a different voice—quiet and gentle—which seemed to flood them with peace.

"Well done, Wakil Ben Abdul," it said. "Your faith has saved not only your apprentice, but also the world from the powers of the evil one."

"Who is it?" whispered Rafi in awe, as both men fell to their knees.

"It's ... it's Marduk ... Allah ... the Infinite One," replied the old man, almost unable to believe what he was seeing. His words were the epitome of reverence.

There was the ghost of a smile in the next words. "You must learn to know me by another name, for I am not Allah. Indeed he and I are opposites, but any oath taken in good faith in his name, as you did and in the name of the powers of good, I take to myself. You now have your apprentice to care for. Live together and learn to love each other."

"Yes ... uh ... Marduk."

"The evil one has been foiled and he will not harm you again. Remember to love. That is my gift ... and my command to you both."

The voice was gone. Only its echo remained in their minds.

Rafi had almost destroyed all existence through his folly and he now looked with new fear at Wakil, but Wakil's face held no anger.

"My poor, poor, Rafi," he whispered, "I was so busy with my own studies and my statesmanship that I completely forgot to instruct you. Come now," he went on, taking the boy's hand, "I must take care of you from now on. You are my apprentice, not my servant and I am your instructor and your friend, not your master."

The two walked back to the house in silence, trying to take in the fact that they had spoken with the Infinite. In times to come, Abdul and Rafi would study together and discover the identity of the strange voice that had spoken to them and their beliefs would undergo a huge change.

Behind them, forgotten on the sand, still open, lay *The Necronomicon*.

The next day, about halfway through the afternoon, Rafi remembered *The Necronomicon* and went back to find it. It was gone. He never saw it again.

* * *

A shadowy figure made its way southwards across the burning sands of Arabia. When it came to a tent, the figure laid a package, which would not be opened for a long time, in a pack belonging to a Bedouin. Then the figure disappeared.

Chapter Three

AD 882
Glastonbury Village, Somerset, England

Merlin the wizard was what he was known as by all those with whom he came into contact. The strange old man knew many things that others did not.

King Arthur Pendragon of Britain, only recently married to the lovely Guinevere, had known of Merlin's power since he was a boy and Merlin had known his father and his grandfather long before.

On this particular day, Arthur and Guinevere along with the Knights of the Round Table and their retainers had left Camelot for the coast of Cornwall to stay at Sir Lancelot's hunting lodge, leaving Merlin to contemplate his old books.

Late that afternoon, Merlin had retired to the rather austere monastery of St. Gregory in Glastonbury nearby, where he gained entrance to the library through the Abbott. Lately, he had been looking at several ancient books, cross-referencing them. As he did, he handled them with reverence, believing these old tomes were worthy of great respect. They were dusty and hard to open and Merlin was afraid of ruining the pages. However, the librarian, Brother Eldred, knew how to handle old pages and carefully opened the books for him.

Merlin was settling himself when he heard a horrible rumbling. It lasted only a few seconds, but in it he heard a terrible longing. Merlin looked up, startled. The monk straightened.

"Brother," asked Merlin, "did you hear anything?"

Brother Eldred looked down at the wizard with a quizzical smile. "My lord?"

"I thought I heard something." Merlin swallowed hard. He recognized the rumble as a prelude to magic: very powerful magic.

Eldred shook his head. "Nay my lord, I heard naught. Would you like a lantern?"

But Merlin was already rising. "No, my brother, I think not. Something is amiss—strangely and terribly amiss," he added, almost as an afterthought. "Pray for me, brother."

The monk looked after him with his mouth open in shock, as Merlin quickly made his way out of the monastery. Brother Eldred swallowed hard. Leaving the books where they lay, he almost ran to the chapel where he knelt and began praying earnestly. Never before had he heard of the great Merlin asking for prayer. Something must be very wrong in the supernatural sphere. The monk prayed even harder.

Merlin hurried into Glastonbury Village toward Camelot, the huge castle that stood out as a great friendly shadow against the purple sky. As the old wizard moved through the village, he noted that the villagers, peasants all, were moving homeward quietly in the time-honoured way, oblivious to the noise. Obviously only those with power could hear it.

As the sun was about to set, he came to the outskirts of the village and stopped, wondering where to go next. Then he heard it again, only this time louder—an evil, triumphant roar with an undertone of anticipation. Merlin turned his head this way and that, trying to pinpoint the direction. Ahead of him lay the fabled castle Camelot. No, it would not be there. There was nobody there anyway, well, nobody of note. Arthur, Guinevere and the Knights had gone southwest to Cornwall and Merlin had checked out the servants and retainers many years before. Behind him lay ancient Glastonbury, Merlin's home for many years, more than even he could remember.

He looked toward where the Brue River lay and thought, *What about that way? No, the noise definitely was not coming from that area.* Merlin paused. Also in that direction lay the home of his friend, Simon the prophet. Merlin thought hard. Simon had power to equal his, but had long before decided to dedicate it all to the Power of Good. Perhaps it might pay to have the Power of Good on his side as well.

He turned and made off toward the river. Even before he came within sight of the house, he saw the bent, aged and wiry form of Simon carrying an unlit lantern and making his way as quickly as possible toward him. When Simon saw the wizard, he cried out in relief and hurried faster. When Merlin reached him, he helped the old man along to a rock.

"Did you hear it?" gasped Simon, sitting heavily.

"Yes and I'm very glad I found you. I was coming to see you. I thought I was losing my mind, but you have confirmed my hearing." Merlin sat down beside the prophet and shook his head. "I wonder what it could be."

"Have you not been able to identify it?" asked Simon anxiously, looking hard into Merlin's face.

Unhappily, the old wizard shook his head. "I have never heard anything like it before. Perhaps," he mentally crossed his fingers and looked at his friend, "uh … you could call on the power of the Infinite?"

"Gladly," replied Simon, brightening, "and I will pray for his help to support your efforts."

Merlin smiled. "Good. But I have not even been able to get a direction on the sound."

"Now there I can help you," replied the elderly prophet, smiling wryly. "I was able to get the direction on the second sounding …"

Simon gasped and covered his ears as the roar burst out again. Merlin went pale and covered his own ears. The sound was so loud that he thought his ears would burst. Finally the noise stopped and the two men, pale and shaken, slowly uncovered their ears.

A passing peasant, chewing on a straw, looked at them curiously as he led his mule homeward. Then shrugging, he moved on. Wizards and wizardry did not concern him. All he was interested in was the pint of beer his wife brewed for him each night.

Meanwhile, the two men had pinpointed the direction—southwest. "So it's off toward the Polden Hills ..." Merlin stopped dead, swallowed hard and looked at Simon. The look on his friend's face told him that the same thought had crossed his mind. Each man looked at the other in horror.

"Morgan le Fay," they both whispered in stunned unison.

* * *

In a clearing, deep in the darkest part of the woods high in the Polden Hills, a fire glowed and a shape danced with wild abandon around the lit area. As it danced, the shadows licked the rocks and cliffs nearby, so that they danced as well.

The shape laughed with glee. "I have it! I have it now! The Book of Dead Names. At last I have *The Necronomicon*. Now I shall have total power over you all."

The evil scroll lay open on the ground nearby. As she danced, Morgan remembered the trials, tribulations and sufferings that she had gone through to find and obtain the blasphemous book. All wizards and witches had heard of the book, of course and most believed it a hoax or fable, but unlike them, Morgan had actually believed in its existence. Finally, after much deliberation, she had decided to attempt to find the tome. It was not long before her considerable powers revealed to her the actual location of the deadly scroll and so she had set out.

The dangerous trip to Arabia took her many miles across the blazing desert to an area near the tiny village of Al-Qalibah. Many times, despite her magic, she had been in fear for her life. The heat of the desert during the day was almost unbearable. Sweat poured off her body at the slightest movement, even though the Arabs seemed not to notice. She couldn't help wondering about the burka-clad women and how they put up with being covered in heavy black in such heat. Nights were freezing and she shivered unhappily as she tried to sleep on the hard sand. Finally, in the Wadi Al-Akhdah, she found the encampment she had seen in her visions.

Almost without thinking, she stuck a knife into the old Arab who owned the scroll, even though he had not even realised what he carried. As she bent to pick up the scroll, a servant walked in on her and immediately shouted the alarm. Morgan's knife was only a second behind, but the man had given her away. As she ran, she could hear shouts and yells behind her.

So began her terrifying flight across the desert—Arabian tribesmen at her heels—alternately running and hiding in fear of her life. She ran horse after horse into the ground on her journey through Palestine, hiding in Jerusalem before fleeing to the coast. She travelled north to the ancient seaport of Joppa and finally found sanctuary in the stinking hold of a rotting ship, which eventually put to sea. To Morgan's dismay, the ship took a grand tour of the Mediterranean, despite the storms that she brought up to try to steer them home.

Morgan was not a good sea traveler and her seasickness, aggravated by the hold's pungent smell, had almost killed her. Finally, after what seemed like an eternity of hell, the ship anchored at the mouth of the Severn River. Her swarthy skin looked deathly pale and she felt more dead than alive. Morgan killed the bo'sun, stole the longboat and desperately rowed ashore. Staggering over the stony beach, she almost kissed the firm ground. She had never been happier in her life. She arrived home five hours later.

Morgan finally stopped dancing and, rubbing her hands together in horrible joy, came back to the scroll. Carefully, she unrolled and smoothed down the first page. Fluent in Arabic, she began to read quickly. Most of the spells she passed over with no more than a cursory glance, not interested in their power. Then she unrolled the next page and her eyes opened wide.

والتنوير المعرفة بقوة الباب فتح

OPENING DOOR OF POWER, KNOWLEDGE AND ENLIGHTENMENT

That was enough. Hurriedly, Morgan moved into her hut to gain the various things required. It only took a few minutes. The evil sorceress who had sold her soul to evil made her way up to a wide open hilltop and quickly made another fire. She prepared the items and assembled the evil altar. Standing in front of the fire and grimacing in horrible glee, she began to intone the dreaded Chant for Opening the Door.

* * *

The roar burst forth again and this time there was no denying the underlying longing, the anticipation. Simon's body forgot it was old and almost ran. He held the lantern high to light their way ahead, but even that light was sometimes not enough. Simon almost collided with a tree twice, but that did not stop him. Merlin was jogging hard to keep up. Morgan's hut was five miles from Glastonbury, high in the Polden Hills through thick woods, a long way in the dark for two old men.

The roar came again and this time the longing was encompassed by a horrible glee. The noise grew and grew. Both men faltered and almost collapsed. Simon flung his lantern arm around his friend's shoulders and, raising the gold cross from around his neck with his other hand, began intoning the Nicene Creed. The roar decreased swiftly as he confessed his belief.

Merlin saw the result of Simon's creed and made up his mind then and there. "Simon," he gasped desperately, "shrive me. Call on the Lord God to forgive me and give me the power and will to carry on."

Simon burst into joyful tears. "Oh, how long I have prayed to hear those words from your mouth. Oh, Merlin, gladly will I pray you, my brother. Kneel with me now. Let the power of the Infinite God of all and his Son cleanse you from your sins and give you the strength of will to complete this task which he has given us."

Prophet and wizard knelt together while Merlin made his confession. As he did so, he was aware of a huge weight lifted from his mind. He began to feel happier than ever before. When the two finally rose to move on, Merlin's steps seemed to float and his mind sing with joy, as they moved on into the darkness of the woods.

Dark storm clouds were gathering as they hurried along and a fork of lightning speared the distant hills followed by the boom of thunder a few seconds later.

Meanwhile, Morgan knew that something was afoot when words began to flow from her mouth totally unbidden. The evil sorceress began to tremble as she reached the last word of the spell and a deathly silence fell. The roar came again, but this time it sounded like words—not in Arabic, but in her own idiomatic Celtic.

"Morgan le Fay, thou has called me. It has been long since I was called."

Morgan pulled herself together. "Who are you?"

"Thou hast read my name in the book," answered the voice. "Now thou must say it. I am Azathoth the all powerful. Thou wouldst have power? Behold, the Door of Power, Knowledge and Enlightenment. Say my name as ye enter. The greatness of eternal youth, total knowledge and limitless power will be thine forever. Come! Come!"

The great, glowing silver path to the doorway stood before her feet. Without hesitation, Morgan stepped onto it and began to stride along it. Then came a panic-stricken shout from behind her.

"Morgan! Morgan! Stop! Please, Stop!"

Turning, she saw two men burst from the forest and hurry up the hillside toward her. It took a few seconds to recognise them as Merlin and Simon. Both men seemed younger somehow, but Morgan did not care. All she wanted was the power that Azathoth had promised.

Merlin stopped so suddenly that Simon collided with him. Following his horrified stare, Simon saw a scroll of parchment manuscript, unbound and unrolled on the ground, its leather thongs lying in disarray. On the unrolled page was a symbol of a five-pointed star with an eye within, clearly visible in the firelight—the Elder Sign. Only one book was old enough to hold that dreaded sign of evil. Merlin gasped.

"Simon, look. That's how she's done it. It's ... oh, by all that's holy ... it's *The Necronomicon*. I've heard about it, but I have never seen it."

Simon paled. "*The Necronomicon?* It can't be. That book is only a myth."

Merlin turned on the man. "Tell that to the book," he shouted, pointing to the scroll. "It's real all right and Morgan is attempting to open the door to hell." He turned to the woman standing on the silver path, sneering at them as she listened to their conversation.

"Morgan, please, for the love of God, stop! Come down. You might just save yourself." His voice shook with fear as horrific pictures of what could happen to his cousin forced themselves into his mind. "You have not the power to control such evil."

She laughed derisively. "You stupid old men, what do you know about power?" She took another step toward the door. "I'll have *all* power when I pass through."

"No, you won't," cried Simon desperately. "That door is evil. You cannot pass through without losing your soul utterly. Surely you, of all people, must realise that."

"No!" shouted Morgan. "You're wrong. It says in *The Necronomicon* that I'll have total knowledge and power over all things when

I pass through the door and say the name."

When she reached the door, she stood on the threshold and hesitated. The two men almost allowed themselves to think she had changed her mind, but she was teasing their hopes. With her hair flailing the air and her eyes open wide in unholy glee, she flung her arms skyward and shrieked at the top of her voice, *"Azathoth!"* Lighting flashed and thunder boomed from the clouds overhead, lighting up her form like a spectre.

Transfixed with horror, the two men stood and stared as the doors swung open. Morgan began to step through, but then she stopped, her body frozen in sudden stark terror. Through the opening she saw a wall of blackness—not just darkness, but total, utter, tangible blackness that tumbled out onto her like a flood. Morgan's body seemed to explode. Her voice shrieked once in unendurable agony, followed by a deathly silence. Then came the roar again, but this time it formed words.

"Merlin! Simon! Ye are too late. Morgan hath done for me what I have waited epochs for. Her soul is mine. Even now she suffereth the eternal agony of the damned. The door to the dark regions is open now. Naught can close it. The armies of evil are loosed. Haaa! Free! Freeeee! Free at last!"

A terrible shape was forming above the door. It first looked like Morgan, but then quickly re-formed as a monstrous, tentacled, indescribable shape, which rose higher and higher until it blocked out the sky above. Merlin could only stand and gape in horror, but Simon suddenly found his mind working with crystal clarity. He felt the Power of Good flowing through him.

"Father God." he whispered, "I am yours. Take me. Use me. I am the channel through which you can work." Fully aware of the enormity of what he was doing, he opened his entire being to the Infinite. Without any action on his part, he felt his arm raise and his finger point at the monster.

"Azathoth. I know you!"

The voice was not his and it was gigantic. It thundered from his throat in a way in which no human voice ever could. The monster hesitated, then roared.

"And I know thee! But thou art too late! I have the whole earth now. No power can e'er take it from me, not even thine."

"**Nay!**" thundered the voice through Simon. **"I can! For did I not create you? You think that I cannot control my own creation? You have your sacrifice, for Morgan gave herself to you because of her greed and because she herself was evil. She was the only one. Avaunt thee, Azathoth!"** Simon's hand raised and formed the sign of the cross in the air. **"Avaunt thee … Satan!"**

With a howl of frustration that seemed to split the very fabric of existence itself, the huge and terrifying shape of Azathoth dissolved and was no more. At that point, Merlin's mind went blank in sheer terror and he sank down in a dead faint.

After a time that could have been measured in microseconds or aeons, Merlin came to and lay there fearfully, wondering what he would see when he opened his eyes. When he did, he found he was still on the darkened hilltop, alongside a dying fire. He scrambled to his feet and looked around. He saw Simon—where he lay dead.

There was a smile on the holy man's face and the body seemed to have a glow around it. There was no sign of the Door to Hell. Merlin looked around and bit his lip in fear; what more could happen? At least the smile on Simon's face made it clear that the old prophet's soul was now at peace.

Without rain the clouds had cleared and now a full universe of stars blazed peacefully down on the old magician. Merlin lifted the old man's body reverently and carried it down the hillside. Simon had sacrificed his life to save his world and his friend. Merlin's tears fell freely on his friend's body as he left. His life would never be the same again. Behind him, forgotten in the darkness and still open, lay *The Necronomicon*.

Later that night, a shape detached itself from the surrounding shadows. It gathered the evil scroll together and retied the leather thongs around it. Raising its arms, it repeated a strange versicle, which was answered in the form of a rumble, like thunder. Then the figure disappeared.

Chapter Four

AD 1146
The Holy Land: The Second Crusade

The armies of the Crusaders were moving across the rain-strewn plains of Turkey, some riding and some—having lost, sold, or eaten their horses—were marching. Nobody, including the kings who were in charge of the whole affair, had made prior arrangements, so whenever food became available, soldiers either took it, killed for it, or paid extortionate prices for it.

Louis VII of France and his fellow king Conrad of Germany were beginning to wonder privately if the trek was worth it. It was quite simply a horrible mess. Footsore, weary and ready to drop, the men finally made it to Anatolia where they hoped to rest. Instead, they found only opposition, sometimes quite ferocious. They were defeated and desperately withdrew. Eventually, the two decimated armies reached Jerusalem, but with so few soldiers remaining, they left the Holy City untouched and headed north.

* * *

Reynald De Chatillon (think, Attila the Hun with attitude) looked up from the floor as the door to the dungeon in Aleppo clanged open.

"Stand!" roared the voice of the jailer and as Reynald stood, the man shouted, "You are to be released. Count yourself lucky. Go!" He stood to one side, leaving the door open.

Unable to believe his good fortune, the knight staggered out into the light for the first time in fifteen years. It felt so good, but as he rode back to his castle of Kerak, his anger grew. How dare they lock him up for all that time. How dare they. He would wreak revenge on the Muslim armies in the years to come; that was for certain.

Arriving at Kerak he sent for his Muslim servants and had them thrown from the battlements. Their screams of despair as they plummeted to certain death, were music to his ears, but this was only the start.

Reynald had put himself at the service first of King Baldwin III of Jerusalem and then of Constance of Antioch. As prince of Antioch, Reynald became even more cruel and violent. He treated the patriarch Aimery with outrageous cruelty to extort money from him. At the instigation of the Byzantine emperor, Manuel I Comnenus, he attacked Armenian Cilicia (southeastern Anatolia), but subsequently he made peace with Thoros II of Cilicia and joined him in an invasion of Byzantine Cyprus.

Manuel had his revenge in 1159 when Reynald was obliged to acknowledge himself as his vassal, but this made no difference to Reynald. He was going to do what *he* wanted to do. The castle strongholds he owned, Kerak and Montreal, controlled Muslim trade routes simply because of their location and although treaties and truces had been signed by both sides, Reynald flagrantly defied them, viciously looting many of the caravans. When asked by no less a person than Saladin himself to restore the plunder, he refused, thus fomenting war. However, like the leaders of the Crusade, he was beginning to wonder if this Kingdom of Jerusalem was all that good an idea.

Late one evening as the sun was just about to set, he stole away to have a think. It was while Reynald was sitting and wondering that he felt a presence. He looked around and saw an Arab standing and watching him.

"Who are you?" demanded Reynald, reaching for his sword.

"My name is Esteban."

"Es … but you are an Arab. How is it that you have a Spanish na … uh …" The man stopped midword, as the other's face seemed to undergo a change. It became a Latin face. They looked at each other quizzically.

"You were saying?"

Reynald shook his head. He must have been mistaken. "Sorry … I … uh …"

"Not at all. You have been thinking, haven't you?"

Reynald nodded.

"I have something here for you. Can you read Arabic?"

"Not all that well, but …"

"Right, then look at this."

The man passed over a strange old scroll, manuscripted on parchment and bound with three leather thongs.

"What is it?"

"I think you might find it interesting. The Arabic name, as you can see," said Esteban as he opened it and unrolled to the first page, "is *Demon Song*. Would you like me to leave it with you?"

"What sort of book is it?"

"A spell book—a very powerful spell book. You might find many of the spells very useful, especially in your present state."

Reynald looked at the opening page. "I see, but what …" He stopped when he realised that Esteban had disappeared.

The evil commander considered reading a little, but deciding that he needed some rest, placed it unopened in his backpack and returned to camp. In the turmoil that passed for daily life in the Crusades, he completely forgot about the strange man and the even stranger scroll.

* * *

The episodes of the Crusade happened and soon things began to pall. Reynald needed something to get rid of the wretched Muslims and one evening he remembered the scroll. After a hunt through his belongings, he located it, but it was in Arabic. Damnation! He was French and his Arabic was poor enough to be utterly useless. However, he knew several of his soldiers could read it and sent for one.

Pedro of Spain appeared before the wicked commander.

"You can read Arabic, I believe?"

"I can, sire."

Reynald indicated a desk behind which stood a chair and on the desk—unrolled to the first page—lay a scroll, manuscripted on parchment with leather thongs attached.

Pedro swallowed and sitting down began to read, "Uh ... *The Book of Dead Names* ... that I have written down in peril of my life."

The man reached the first spell. "I cannot read this, sire." He went on, "I am afraid for my life."

Reynald glared at the man. "You will take the scroll into the desert close by and read it to me there. If anything goes wrong, it will be your fault."

Trembling with horror, Pedro bundled up the scroll. He walked outside onto the Palestinian desert, spread it out on the sandy ground and continued to read. The strange words seemed to pronounce themselves as he read down the page.

Reynald stood there watching. He was quite sure that he could take care of anything that happened.

"All right, stop," he commanded. "Go to the top of the next page and start again."

The spell finished at the bottom of the page. Pedro breathed a sigh of relief and began to read again from the top of the following page. Eventually he reached a certain page and read, "Opening the Door of Power, Knowledge and Enlightenment."

"Ah," said Reynald, his face lighting up. This was what he wanted—total power. Yes. "Continue on," he commanded.

"Sire, there are some preparations which need to be made."

"Then make them, you idiot—now!"

Feeling just a little offended, Pedro hurried back to camp and after some searching, found the various items required. He hurried back to Reynald and quickly set up. Then trembling with utter fear, he began to pronounce the dreaded words of the spell.

Reynald was feeling more and more exhalted. He had wanted total power his whole life and now here it was.

Pedro was feeling the power flowing through him, terrifying him even more. The words were saying themselves in his mouth even as he spoke. He finished the spell and sat gasping, wondering what was going to happen.

He and Reynald were stunned when they heard a thunderous voice come from nowhere.

"Reynald!" it roared, *"I know thee!"*

Swallowing hard, Pedro was about to speak when Reynald waved him to silence. The evil man addressed the empty air. "All right, who are you and where have you come from?"

"My name is Azathoth and I am from the outer circles. I have power that you can have. Behold the Door to Ultimate Power."

The silver path and the great door appeared and the two men gaped in amazement.

"Thou hast only to say my name as thou crosses the threshold of The Great Door," roared the voice of the spirit. *"The name thou must say is Azathoth! Come!"*

"Oh God of all, please send help," gasped Pedro and he collapsed on the sand, despair overwhelming him.

Then as if to answer his desperate prayer, a Muslim warrior on a horse crossed a nearby hill and came toward them. No ordinary person, the figure drew its sword and roared, "In the name of Allah, I defy you, Shaitan and command you to leave!"

The monster roared, but found itself once again foiled and the door and path disappeared. The man turned his horse and approached the two men. It was none other than the great Saladin himself. In desperation, Petro turned and ran for his life. The poor man raced back to his tent, gathered a few things he thought he might need, then began the long trek home. He was never seen again, but rumors say that he found his way to Tibet and changed his spiritual outlook. He became a monk and stayed in Tibet until the end of his days.

After Petro fled, the Arab jumped from his horse uncoiling a rope as he landed. Reynald found himself bound and cursed the other, but Saladin smiled. He was a very gentle man, but such awesome evil he could *not* stand. At last he held captive the wickedest Crusader captain. He rode slowly away, dragging Reynald with him. Reynald had no other option but to follow.

That evening, in the darkness, a figure approached *The Necronomicon* as it lay on the ground. It gathered up the evil book. Then the figure disappeared.

* * *

For three days the two made their way over burning sands until they reached Jerusalem. By this time, Reynald was very fearful. He had no idea what Saladin was planning for him or what he was going to do to him.

Saladin tied up Reynald in his tent just outside the Dung Gate for about a week to let him stew. When he returned with a razor-sharp, Arab scimitar (Arabs knew how to sharpen scimitars), Reynald, showing his true cowardly colours, wept and pleaded.

After making him confess all his crimes inexcruciating detail, which took almost four hours, Saladin kicked Reynald in the gut and he bent over in pain. Saladin raised his scimitar and in one blow cut off Reynald's head.

* * *

Several years later, Uther De Halifax—soldier of the Crusades, who had served the Kingdom of Jerusalem for as long as it lasted—passed away. His friends, who loved him dearly, had decided to give him a huge send-off until it came to light that he didn't want one. All he wanted was to be left in peace in a simple tomb in one of the caves by the Dead Sea.

So that is what they did. The old man was left there—seemingly forever.

Chapter Five

AD 1490
Madrid, Spain

* * *

Over three hundred years later, Uther De Halifax's sarcophagus remained in peace and darkness in a cave near the Dead Sea where his fellows had placed it. The interior was dry and cool.

A figure drew near in the darkness and, with difficulty, shifted the stone cover about a foot to the side. A singular item—an old parchment scroll bound with three leather thongs was placed alongside the corpse. The figure stared hard at the face of the knight, slid the cover back and disappeared.

All was silent again.

* * *

On his huge, cushioned throne sat the grossly fat, disgustingly ugly, utterly repulsive figure of Cardinal Delgado[1] of Spain (think Jabba the Hutt's ugly brother after a night of debauchery). As Inquisitor General of the Spanish Inquisition—resplendent in full red-white-and-green robes trimmed with ermine—he was responsible for overseeing the scene of horror in the dungeon before him.

He had thought of taking a biblical name as most priests did, but wanting his own name to last forever, he decided against it. He had

---

[1] Rather ironic that Delgado means Thin Man.

a look that was not entirely rational and his right eye was lazy, so one was never sure where he was looking. The man's lips never quite met and there was a permanent line of drool marking his jawline. Altogether, he was a very nasty sort of person.

He took a guzzle of wine from the golden goblet in his right hand, spilling some down his already badly stained robes and licked the fleshy thick lips that covered rotten and decaying teeth. He would never admit to anyone that the pain and suffering he witnessed gave his sadistic mentality a feeling of sheer ecstasy. So far this morning, there had been four so-called witches who had been put to "The Question, Both Ordinary and Extraordinary," and their broken and mangled bodies lay in a heap on the edge of the room, ready to be taken out of the city and cast into the lime pits. Whether they were innocent or guilty was of no interest to him; he only wanted to hear the shrieks and screams of agony, terror and horror, which he found so exciting.

He had watched the other priests having their own bit of fun with two young and pretty female witches, raping them mercilessly before they were tortured; they found it so entertaining. Of course, as priests they were not supposed to enjoy such sinful things, but since they gave each other absolution as soon as they were finished, it was all right. Delgado had not joined in. He preferred little boys to women, the younger the better.

It was the total power over life and death that turned Delgado on the most. Knowing he could condemn a human to death by protracted horrendous torture simply with a wave of his fat, beringed hand was his thing. That was his greatest pleasure—to see the sheer terror and horror of those condemned. Delgado smiled remembering. He had been offered a rulership of several kingdoms throughout Europe and had he taken one, he could have become an emperor. But why take that temporal power when as the inquisitor general, he wielded far more power.

Now the priests below him were dealing with a certain Barrett

Muerte, who had been denounced as a devil worshipper by one of the Inquisition's spies and was, therefore, brought before the so-called justice of the church. The priests had chosen the rack for the man and at the moment that Delgado brought his mind back, Barrett's body was being stretched hard as he shrieked in agony. Delgado smiled cruelly as he descended from the throne to better witness the evil his priests were doing.

Picking up a vial of holy water, he sprinkled it on the man's body and said a quick prayer for appearances. Then he drew near to the rack. "Will you confess your sin of worshiping the Dark One?" he cried, waving away Father Bartholomew and taking the handle himself. "Fling yourself on the mercy of the church and the Holy Virgin. You may then be able to save your immortal soul." He twisted the handle over cruelly.

Barrett's eyes bulged out and the sweat poured off his body as his limbs were stretched horribly. "You don't know what you are talking about," he shrieked. "I know of more power than you will ever have."

Delgado blinked. "What do you mean about power?"

A ghost of a crafty look came over the man's face and he turned to the cardinal.

"You don't know what it is, do you? No, of course not. You think that because you have power over many people in this world, you have total power." The man's voice rose to a cry. "You are wrong. *Ha.* You are totally wrong. I and only I know where total power may be gained."

Father Mark, a priest who enjoyed using glowing brands, stepped forward with his weapon of choice in his hand and brought it close to the man's groin. "How dare you address my lord cardinal so. In the name of God, you will suffer for this outrage."

He drew back his hand, about to make good his threat when Delgado stayed his hand. The cardinal's voice was soft and infinitely sinister. "Tell me more. Tell me all. Tell me now, or you will suffer as you have never suffered before."

Barrett turned his head to the cardinal, looked at him squarely and spoke quietly, "There is a book in a far off place. It and *only* it, has the spells and chants to give a human total power over the universe."

Normally the inquisitor would have given no thought to such terror-stricken ramblings; he heard such statements as part of confessions every day, but something in the man's manner—a certain arrogance—made him take notice. Delgado swallowed and licked his lips. Total power over the universe. What wouldn't he give for that.

"My Lord," remarked Father Mark, driving his brand deep into the red-hot coals of the brazier to reheat it, "this blasphemer and heretic must be saved from the power of evil. We must continue."

"No," retorted Delgado, loudly. "We will pursue this person in our private chambers. Have him taken down."

To the surprise of the priests, the man was dragged away, followed by Delgado who waved at them to continue. As he walked out, he could hear a woman's voice pleading in terror as she was dragged into the torture chamber and her rags ripped off. Then her screams took on a higher note as she was brutally violated. Delgado regretted that he would not be participating in her "salvation," but he reasoned that a little withdrawal now might soon give him—he licked his lips in obscene longing—the whole world's population cringing in fear at his beck and call, forever. Delgado smiled craftily, obscenely imagining long lines of little boys—crying in terrified, horrified anticipation—waiting for him to beat, ravish and torture them to his heart's content and their parents chained up on the side of the dungeon, looking helpless as mothers wept or screamed in agony and fathers cursed in rage. He could hardly wait.

Then he wiped his face clean and put on his best pious expression as he entered his study where Father Dominic and Father Luke stood on each side of the broken body of the young man.

Barrett looked up at the evil, sadistic, pedophiliac cardinal and smiled wryly. "I thought you would be interested in the possibility of total power." He was apparently feeling no pain at all now.

Delgado stiffened and gritted his teeth as he turned to Friar Manuel, the scribe, who was just lifting his quill to record the proceedings. "This is not to be recorded. Nor shall it be remembered. It shall be forgotten."

Nodding, Manuel laid down his pen.

"And cover him up. We don't want to look at his naked body," *at least, not yet.*

He turned to Barrett as Luke flung a robe at the man. "You, my—*amigo*, will now tell me all about this so-called book of power. You will tell me all. Where it is to be found. What it has to say. And be warned, *señor*," Delgado's voice sank to the most sinister whisper, "if you have lied, you will suffer such agony as will be spoken about in whispers for many thousands of years. We have ways of keeping you alive and screaming for months. Believe me when I tell you we will give you plenty of cause to scream and when death does come, you will welcome it with open arms."

"Oh, don't worry, milord, I have spoken the truth and I will tell you," replied Barrett dragging the robe around his skinny frame. "In fact," the man seemed struck with an idea, "if you will allow, I can show you where to find it. It is almost impossible to describe the place."

"Where is it?" In spite of his efforts to conceal, Delgado's face showed his eagerness.

"Palestine, on the shore of the Dead Sea. It's in a cave in the cliffs."

Delgado swallowed and looked at the two priests. It seemed too easy. Why had not the man attempted to make some sort of bargain? Perhaps it was a sign that, indeed, the man was speaking the truth. Finally, Delgado came to a decision.

"All right, we shall go, all four of us, to Palestine, but be warned;

if you are lying, you will suffer agonies worse than those of the eternally damned."

"Oh, it's there all right," murmured Barrett, a faint enigmatic smile on his face.

* * *

The darkness of the knight's tomb was almost total—seeming to fulfill his wish for all eternity—except for a lighted torch that burned in the darkness as four human figures approached. One stepped forward. "There it is. It's …"

The last man in line interrupted, "All right. Stand aside and wait. Do not move."

"Just a minute," retorted the first, "I want to …"

"You cannot," roared the other. "You have done your part in the aiding of Mother Church. Now do as you are told." The other's voice became sneeringly condescending. "I may even consider allowing you … to live."

It had taken almost four months to plan and make the trip, as everything had to be done in strictest secrecy. Now after trekking the full length of the Mediterranean Sea on the old pilgrim road, they had finally arrived at the cave to the east of the Dead Sea and found the knight's tomb. The two priests stepped forward and with great difficulty hove the lid off the sarcophagus. It fell to the ground with a dull thud.

Cardinal Delgado noted vaguely the presence of an imperfectly preserved corpse with a red cross over the heart and a shield tucked alongside it. But he only had eyes for the object within the grasp of the body's hands. Almost drooling in anticipation, he reached in and carefully took the scroll. Placing it on the floor, he untied the thongs and unrolled it, scanning the first page. *Damn! It's in Arabic.*

"Read it to me if you are able," he demanded of the priests beside him.

Father Dominic squinted at the parchment in the dull light and began to pick out the characters. After puzzling over them for a minute or so, he looked up at the cardinal. "I am afraid my Arabic is very poor, my lord, but I think it says … er … the two opening words are obviously a title. It reads … er …" His brow furrowed as he tried to read the Arabic characters. Then he paused and gave a self-deprecating guffaw. "Oh my, I am a fool. Arabic reads right to left, not left to right. One moment, my lord."

Starting at the right of the page, he began again—tracing the various Arabic characters with a finger.

"*Uh* … Demon Song … Scroll of … .Black Earth … Dead … Labels? That must mean names … written … in … er … danger? No, peril of … life. So it says, er … '*Scroll of Dead Names.*' *Uh*, that sounds familiar, 'which I have written in peril of my li …' Oh no."

The man gasped in frightful shock when he recognised the lines. What priest did not know those fabulous, shocking words? He looked up at his master, his face white with terror, "My lord, it's … it's Abdul Al-Hazred's *Necronomicon*."

Delgado nodded. He had recognised the opening words as well. So that was what Muerte was on about. No wonder he spoke about total power. This scroll contained unbelievable possibilities. His face pale, he motioned the other to continue. Trembling, Dominic was about to attempt it, when he suddenly became aware that they were one short. When he looked around, he saw that Barrett Muerte was nowhere to be seen.

A strangled cry broke his reverie and he looked over at Father Luke, the second priest, whose face was blanched white in the light of the torch and whose trembling finger pointed at the corpse. Even though the vicissitudes of the cave had wrought their worst upon the body, the face was still recognizable as that of Barrett Muerte. Now firmly convinced that Barrett had been a ghost or worse, the two priests trembled harder in their terror.

To Delgado, this was of no consequence now that he had the book. That was all that mattered. The evil cardinal quickly rolled up the scroll, tied it carefully and stowed it in his carrier bag.

"We will return to Spain and I shall make a study of this book."

"My lord, I beg of you," cried Dominic, "do not attempt to cast the spells in the book. You must realise how evil they are—evil beyond all comprehension."

Delgado smiled. "You may leave the book with me. I shall …" The man smiled mirthlessly. "Take care of it."

Luke swallowed hard and looked over at Dominic with terrified eyes.

* * *

After the three left and the cave was silent and in darkness once again, a familiar figure stepped out of the shadows .He looked down at the face of the dead knight and chuckled.

"Thanks for the use of your face, old friend. Once they translate the scroll—who knows—my dread master may soon rule the world once again. Perhaps not, but it matters not, for I have much time on my hands. One thing is for sure: Cardinal Delgado will answer for the pain and suffering he wrought on my person." The man snarled. "Oh yes, one way or another, he will pay an infinite number of times over."

With a wicked laugh, the strange man stared hard at the old knight's face and his own lost Uther's Latin visage and became the swarthy, handsome, evil, Arabic face of Nyarlathotep.

As Barrett he had played on the torture he had undergone, making it look as if he could not move without help, but he was just feeling lazy. In truth, he could move as well as anyone. He had, in times past, undergone far worse than these pathetic individuals could inflict. For example, he remembered with a wry smile, he had even been crucified by the Romans for robbery about one thousand three hundred years ago, alongside two other men at the top of a hill just outside Jerusalem, only forty or so miles from where he now stood. He had been bored, so to pass the time he fell in with a robber band in the hills alongside Jericho. Roman soldiers caught them during their fourth escapade and dragged them back to Jerusalem. Although Roman law demanded that a person be tried fairly, it only referred to Roman citizens. All others were automatically considered guilty. The two had been beaten to within an inch of their lives, then flung into jail to await their fate.

One day, they were joined by another man and they all had to carry their crosses by the crossbars to a nearby hill. When they reached it, they were nailed to the wood and raised up. He could still remember it—indeed he didn't think he would ever forget it. Oh, the agony from the pain of nails through his wrists and heels and also in his back. He had cursed and reviled everyone, including the one in the middle—the new fellow—but that worthy somehow managed to hold his peace beyond several sentences, which made no sense to Nyarlathotep's pain-blasted brain.

The thief on the opposite side had shouted out, "Be quiet you fool. We are getting our just desserts, but this man has done nothing wrong." He then looked at the man in the centre and said something very strange. "Lord, remember me when you come to your kingdom."

The other had replied, "This day you will be with me in paradise."

Nyarlathotep shook his head and thought, *What a lot of rot*. He remembered that the man had words with another man and two women who approached him, but Nyarlathotep could not hear what he said.

Before long, the man said, "It is finished," and then he passed away.

The sky clouded over and then came several crashes of thunder, but no rain. Some women and two elderly men, who looked a bit like priests, took down the man's body, bearing it away almost reverently. Nyarlathotep couldn't understand why; the man was quite ordinary as far as he was aware and normally any crucified crook was left on the cross to rot. *Strange.*

It wasn't until twenty years later that he found out just who the man was. Over the following centuries he watched in amazement as a religion surrounding this man grew into a world-encompassing belief. Who would have thought that a simple carpenter could grow a huge, powerful religion? Perhaps ... he wasn't just a carpenter.

The Roman soldiers had come about an hour later and broken their knees to hasten their deaths. The other man had died gasping and screaming, almost within the hour. Nyarlathotep hung there in awesome agony through two thunderstorms and freezing nights for another three days, his throat raw with screaming. Many Jews passed by, reviling him for making a fuss during the Jewish Sabbath, but by this time he was beyond caring.

To his surprise, the nail through his right wrist came loose during the second night. The Roman executioner was not the best. With a desperate wriggle and heave he pulled out the other nails and his emaciated, tortured body had fallen. Happily he didn't break any more bones, which would have been even more catastrophic for him.

After lying there for an hour or so, desperately trying to recover, he had crawled away and eventually made his escape into the Judean countryside. There was no way he could walk with broken kneecaps, so he had hidden during the day and crawled on during the night. Eventually, after five days of desperate crawling and hiding, he had found a cave deep in the wilderness. In its depths he found sanctuary where he could relax, but it was almost impossible with the pain he felt. He had desperately managed to remain silent during the agonising saga, but now he could let himself go. The cave rang with his cries of agony.

Being immortal, he didn't need food. After about three months, the wounds healed to a point where he could handle the pain. It took almost three years before the pain disappeared completely. Many times during those dreadful years of agony he had prayed for the reaper's kiss, but it never came and he had to make the best of things. He looked down at the tiny, almost unnoticeable holes in his wrists. They had, in spite of several painful infections, eventually healed completely and were now painless. Occasionally, he still had trouble moving his hands and, every now and again, his knees would give him gyp and cause him to limp.

Compared to his torture on the cross, his time in the Inquisition's torture chamber was almost a walk in the park. The Romans sure knew how to torture.

With a laugh that was utterly devoid of humour, the evil keeper of the scroll covered up the knight and vanished.

Uther De Halifax, knight and soldier of the Crusades, was left alone once again—this time for eternity.

* * *

Some days later in the church of St. Michael, in the tiny village of Ubeda in Southern Spain, a young priest had finished morning Mass and was just beginning his prayers when a messenger arrived on horseback and came running in.

"Father Matthew, I come with a message from Cardinal Delgado of Madrid. He bids you attend him as soon as you can and bring your Arabic texts."

Father Matthew, whose real name was Oleus Wormus, had taken the apostle's name when he became a priest. Upon hearing the message, he stiffened. He knew Delgado; indeed, who did not know the inquisitor general? Matthew wondered what the Cardinal wanted with him. After a moment, he turned to the messenger.

"All right, bear the following message to his holiness. Tell him I shall kiss his ring in two days." Matthew hesitated, then added, "Bear also my highest regards to his holiness." He smiled wryly; *a little crawling does no harm, especially with one so powerful.*

"Yes, Father," replied the messenger. Bowing, he ran from the room.

With a sigh, Matthew knelt and prayed for guidance. When he stood, he called in Deacon José and charged him with keeping his parish until he returned. Then gathering his Arabic texts and binding them together, he took a small pack of food, mounted his mule and rode off in the direction of Madrid.

Delgado was seated on his throne when Matthew walked through the door two days later. The Cardinal looked sardonically at the younger priest as the worthy bowed to kiss his superior's ring.

"Very glad you could come, Father Matthew," he said, sounding anything but glad. "I need your wisdom to translate a scroll I have acquired from Palestine."

In spite of himself, Matthew found himself blurting out, "I thought it was in Arabic, not Hebrew."

Delgado smiled as he rose to his feet and beckoned the other to follow. "It is. It was found in a cave near the Dead Sea and I want to know what it says."

"Very well, my lord," replied Matthew, his curiosity aroused as he followed the Cardinal into his study. "What is this scroll?"

"You have no doubt heard of it before. It is called …" Delgado paused for effect, then deliberately rolled the name off his tongue, "*The Necronomicon*."

Matthew stopped dead and his jaw dropped. "No," he whispered, "it cannot be."

Delgado looked around and nodded. "It is and if you cannot—or *will not* translate, I will find someone who will. You will then find yourself," his voice sank to a whisper, "without a parish, without a job, without a religion and *without a soul*. Do I make myself clear?"

Matthew's face had gone white. Swallowing hard, he nodded. The man had a way of making himself perfectly understood. Matthew followed the cardinal into his study where a young friar—with parchment, quill and ink—was already seated. This worthy stood as the two entered.

"Father Matthew, may I introduce Friar Philip," said Delgado shortly. The two nodded to each other. "You, Father will translate," said the cardinal, looking at Matthew, "and you," he continued, looking at Philip, "will write—in Latin. Leave out naught. Add naught. Your writing shall be clear. It shall be easily read. If not … ." The evil Cardinal let the unspoken threat hang in the air and Philip's face paled.

He nodded and sat down, dipping his goose-feather quill and holding it poised over the parchment as Matthew settled himself.

Delgado passed over the leather-bound scroll and smiled as Matthew handled it with what looked like loathing. Then he quickly went off to his private chambers to join a young lad he was *very* interested in …

The young priest untied the thongs and opened the scroll to the first page, his own Latin and Arabic texts open alongside. He did not need them to read the main title: *Al Azif; Demon's Song, The Necronomicon*; The Book of Dead Names," he rattled off and the friar's pen flew over the page. "Written by Abdul Al-Hazred. Translation by …" Father Matthew paused and then shrugging, decided to put his proper name to the translation, "Oleus Wormus."

Philip looked at him, eyebrows raised.

"'Tis my common name. Something as important as this should have the real name attached. All right, first paragraph: Introduction. Start." He looked at the next phrase and switched from Spanish to Latin, which all educated men could read at that time, "*Ecce liber terra nigram, liber necro nomica est, ego in periculus salus meo conscribero …*"

Slowly, over the next twelve days, the two worked carefully over the faded Arabic text. When they came to writing the spells, Matthew carefully spelled them out, making sure not to say a single word and Philip carefully wrote them down. They trembled with fear while translating, waiting for the bolt of lightning, which would signal God's wrath at such horrific blasphemy, or worse, the spell to be cast, with utterly catastrophic consequences. To their sheer relief, no such thing happened and after two weeks of hard work, they had translated the whole of the tome.

And what a tome it was. In spite of his horror while doing the work, Matthew had to admire the unknown Arab's industry, for the words were written in such a way as to denote a love of the language and, indeed, a love for life itself. Written Arabic is a pretty language, lending itself readily to calligraphy and sometimes Al-Hazred had used embellishments in his writing that were—quite frankly—beautiful. *On the other hand*, thought Matthew, *if that was the case, how come he wrote so much blasphemy?* Was it because, as was commonly thought, the man was utterly insane? It had been stated in other writings that Al-Hazred was quite mad, but this did not look like the work of a madman. Matthew puzzled over these anomalies during the few hours per day the two men allowed themselves rest and refreshment.

When the full translation was finally finished, the men shuddered, as others had done before them, when they saw the incomplete last page. The long inked line whipped across the parchment told of a horrifying finish. There was no sign-off or lineage by the author, which had been common in those days.

"*Ecce libre slavus deii* … and then that line," finished Matthew, "Goodness knows what caused it."

The two men looked at each other and shook their heads in sorrow and wonder.

Once the last word was written, priest and friar quickly bound the finished sheets into a rough book, then held a short Mass, thanking God for their safety during this terrifying ordeal and asking a blessing for them in whatever was to come. Both were convinced that Delgado would not let them go and they would end up in the chamber of the Question. What they would be accused of they had no idea, but they knew that the inquisitor would trump up some fake charge.

Then Philip had an idea. He had been scribe in the castle for almost a year and knew of a back door, carefully hidden, that he had come across totally by accident a month or so before. Leaving book and scroll lying side by side and breathing a prayer for protection, the two men got up. After checking that the coast was clear, they put their hoods over their heads and tried to look inconspicuous as they trudged slowly down the corridor. That walk seemed to take forever and their hearts were in their mouths as they passed door after door.

One closed door had the cardinal's personal coat of arms on it which denoted it as his private quarters. As they passed, they could hear screaming and crying in a young boy's voice, accompanied by what sounded like cane whippings. They could also smell the remains of an old meal wafting from the door. The rotting-meat smells were disgusting. Shaking their heads, they hurried on.

As they turned the corner, the door opened and the huge shape of the cardinal waddled out. They had only just missed him. The door slammed behind him and he disappeared toward the study.

The two desperately kept themselves from hurrying. Several times other monks, friars and priests passed them, but they were unchallenged and finally arrived at an alcove. Entering, Philip went straight to an unremarkable tapestry alongside a bookcase, drew it back and discovered the door they sought. As silently as they could manage, they opened it. It crunched and squealed as it ground against the stonework, making them swallow hard. Fortunately, nobody was listening and after a moment, they exited. The door grated closed and the tapestry fell back into place.

They hurried away, every moment expecting to hear Delgado's horrible voice shouting for them to come back, but nothing happened and they made their escape.

* * *

Delgado entered the study and found the parchment, together with the completed translation, lying on the study desk. He saw no sign of the two clerics and after some searching, he shook his head. *Damn*. He had been looking forward to condemning the pair to the torture chamber and torturing them for weeks. He cursed them both, but at least he had the book. He slathered, looking forward to what he could gain by its use.

The evil cardinal returned to the study and quickly wrapped the original scroll in oilcloth and placed it in a wooden box. He wrapped it again in oilcloth, poured melted tallow over it and set his seal on it. Although he didn't have to, this had become a habit. When it had set and was air and water tight, he took it down into the deepest dungeon—the *oubliette* (French for forgotten) so named because a prisoner could be locked there and forgotten. In the damp layers of earth under a flagstone, he dug a hole and placed the scroll in the dry clay at the bottom of the hole. He covered it over and replaced the stone.

Later, he left instructions that he was not to be disturbed, sat down at his desk and opened the Latin translation.

At about the same time, some fifteen miles away, Matthew and Philip had stopped at The Galleon, a wayside inn, for the night. They had finished eating a good meal and were enjoying a glass of wine in preparation for turning in.

"I am very glad that is over," said Philip.

Matthew grinned wryly. "I agree." Then he grew thoughtful. "But brother, I invite your thoughts—that man who wrote those words down surely must have known what he was writing."

"Indeed. I do not understand," replied Philip. "His writing seemed quite lucid, did it not? The writing was quite readable, right up to the last page. No madman would have written like that, especially the beautiful flourishes in the Arabic, but the content of the writing—*whew*. Surely, neither Christian nor indeed any man of goodwill—whatever his beliefs—should be allowed to use such power, for spells are supposed to give total power over all. My good friend Brother Andrew said that power corrupts and absolute power corrupts absolutely."

Matthew nodded. "That crossed my mind too. There is considerable discrepancy between the writing and the content." The man shook his head in wonder.

"Unless …" Philip stroked his chin.

Matthew raised his eyebrows.

"Well, perhaps, just supposing." the young friar took a deep breath and faced his deepest fears, "he did not actually realise what he was writing?"

"But he must have."

Philip paused, thinking. Then he raised his eyebrows. "Don't forget there are many types of madness, some of which we don't know about and possibly will never know."

Matthew started to speak but caught himself. There was indeed just that possibility. "But if that is the case then the spells could be for some things which are totally different. For instance, that big one that is supposed to open the door to all knowledge, power and enlightenment may not be for that at all."

"Then … what is it for?" Philip's face paled as he phrased the question.

"Well, the words of the spells that I saw are phonetic, not actual Arabic. I think they could be ancient Sumarian. So their meaning is totally unknown. The spell could be for anything—raising demons, or even … er …"—the priest swallowed hard—"opening the Door to Hell."

"No!" Philip's eyes opened wide in shock and his voice was a wild whisper. "We did not find out what M'lord Delgado was intending to do with the translation. If he tries to cast any of the spells, he and possibly the whole world could be in the greatest danger. We must warn him."

Matthew looked sideways at the young man with a wry smile. "I admire your loyalty, Philip, but perhaps it would be better to let the man be." He mused, entertaining the ironic and slightly irreligious thought that if the evil inquisitor general should happen to open the Door to Hell, he would be most welcome to it and maybe he'd even fall in.

But Philip shot to his feet and glared at the other. "What kind of thought is that for a devout, pious Christian? How dare you, *señor*. It is our avowed duty to serve our Mother Church at the cost of our lives if it may be. We must go back and tell him."

Matthew patted the air with his hands. "All right, brother, all right. I apologize and beg your forgiveness. Please be seated and finish your wine and we will have a good night's rest. Then, on the morrow, we shall go back and tell him. But," he said as he swallowed hard, "I don't give much for our lives when we do."

Philip simmered down and swallowed. "All right. So be it. My prayers shall indeed be fervent this night."

"Mine, too."

"All right, let us sleep now and we will begin our return at first light."

But neither man slept well. They were scared—very scared about what the evil man would do when they tried to tell him about their thoughts

* * *

Deep in the castle a light burned all night ...

* * *

"Open! Open! Ho, guard, open!" cried a voice, waking the guard with a start. Shaking his head to try and clear it of slumber, he rose from his seat inside the barred door and looked out. Two men stood outside, both looking apprehensive. They had found by experiment that the back door could not be opened from without, so taking their lives in their hands, they had approached the main gate.

Murmuring a prayer for forgiveness, the guard quickly opened the gate. "Reverend *señors* both, I beg your forgiveness for my laxity. I was …"

Matthew burst in. He was beyond accusing the man and quickly blessed him with a sign of the cross in the air. Then he took a deep breath. "My Lord Cardinal Delgado, is he within?"

The guard blinked. "Nay, he left almost two hours ago while the sun was yet still down. The sun has since risen."

Matthew breathed a sigh of relief. "Was he on his own?"

"*Si.*"

"On foot?"

"*Si.*" The guard wore a wry grin. No donkey or horse could carry the bloated man's weight, at least a hundred and sixty kilos.

The two men looked at each other and swallowed hard. With the immediate terror of being thrown into the torture chamber alleviated, they suddenly found themselves fearing for the world.

Matthew pushed the guard aside and strode down five corridors to the study where he and Philip had worked so industriously. Since nobody else was aware of what they had been translating, they knew they were safe. Several priests looked at the two as they passed, but there was such a look of intention on their faces they did not intervene.

As the guard had said, there was no sign of Delgado, *The Necronomicon*, or the translation. Rubbing his chin, Matthew hurried along the corridors with Philip hot on his heels and finally found the Cardinal's private rooms, where they had heard the boy screaming. Normally they would never even dare to trespass on such a private area, but this was an emergency. They pushed the door open and peered in.

There was no sign of the man or the translation. There was, however, a young lad of no more than ten, tied and lying face down on a bare pallet, sobbing and obviously in pain. Dried blood was caked around the boy's buttocks and many bruises from a cane marked the whole of the boy's back. He had been beaten mercilessly and violated repeatedly.

Matthew ground his teeth in anger as he took in the disgusting and disgraceful results of Delgado's perversion. "What is your name, lad?" he asked gently.

The boy raised his head quickly and looked at them through horror-filled eyes, obviously expecting more torture, but when he saw the priest's kindly eyes he swallowed and said, "J–Juan, *señor*."

"Where is the cardinal?" asked Philip, quickly untying the boy.

Juan shook his head, rubbing his bruised wrists. "He left me alone here yesterday and told me not to s–s–stir," he sobbed. "He said he would be coming back for me. I don't know where he went." Juan rubbed his lacerated buttocks gently, wincing in pain.

"Did he take anything with him?"

"I do not know."

"What has he done with them?" gasped Philip, his fear intensifying.

"He must have taken them with him. The guard may have seen which way he went," replied Matthew.

When he was about to go out to question the guard, something made him quickly run into Delgado's private chapel next door and pick up two of the Host wafers from the ciborium on the altar.

"Why have you taken them?" asked Philip.

"Spiritual protection." replied Matthew tersely. *But*, he thought, *since they have been blessed by such an evil man, they may not be any protection at all. We will have to trust to fortune.*

Then he turned to Juan who had joined them. The lad was swallowing hard, obviously still terrified and wondering what was going to befall him now. He was skinny and badly malnourished. Philip, trying hard to ignore the rotting meat and other food there, quickly grabbed a loaf of bread from the cardinal's table. He handed it to the boy, who tore into the bread—almost choking.

"Be careful. Don't eat so fast or you'll endanger yourself."

Nodding, Juan slowed his chewing.

"All right, lad, go home to your family and thank God you are still alive. I don't think you will ever come back here again. *Dimitas in pace* (Go in peace)." Matthew said, blessing him with a sign of the cross over his head.

The boy's jaw dropped in disbelief. Hardly daring to believe his good fortune, he quickly hurried to the bedroom, flung a convenient robe around his body and hurried back. Philip led him to the back door behind the tapestry.

Still chewing the loaf, Juan whispered, "Thanks, *señor* and bless you." He gave the man a hug and in the next moment, took to his heels and was gone.

The inquisitor's priests had plucked Juan and his two friends Sanchez and José from the road almost four weeks before. Along with several other boys, they were made to undergo horrors that no one would wish on a worst enemy. His friends had died screaming in agony and despair under the continuous torturous perversions and he himself had long since given up the idea of escape, resigning himself to his fate at the hands of the evil cardinal.

Thanking everything holy for the reprieve, the boy hurried away. After walking a mile or so, he came across a slow-moving stream that formed a little swimming hole close by. Throwing off his robe and dumping the remains of the bread on top, he plunged into the clear, cleansing water. His open wounds stung, but the water soothed them. Oh, how good it felt.

He drank long and deep from the stream's clean water and thought that he had never tasted water so good. He donned his robe, finished the bread and made off to the east. He managed after considerable searching to find his way back to his rural family, four miles out of Madrid, who were very pleased to see him. He didn't stir from his family's home for the rest of his life, but sadly in the years to come, he often woke crying in horror as nightmare after nightmare of his time at the hands of the cardinal assailed his sleep. He refused point-blank to attend Mass ever again and when the angelus bell sounded from the local church, he refused to stop to pray; he simply spat and cursed and went on with his work.

If a priest visited with the usual dire threats of excommunication, purgatory and eternal damnation, he grabbed whatever weapon he could reach and with shouts of "I'll see you in hell then." took to the man, sometimes beating him so thoroughly that the other could hardly walk. He was permanently scarred, never married and died a bitter, disenchanted atheist at the age of thirty-seven.

His parents and siblings were shocked at his actions, but when they heard his horrifying tale, they also gave up religion, refusing to stop to pray at the angelus or attend Mass. All of them were excommunicated from the church, but it made no difference to them and in spite of dreadful persecution, they persevered.

Four hundred years later, after the Reformation, their descendants took Plato's teaching of "truth being found from reason rather than dogma" and founded the "Rationalist" movement—a movement of atheism, which has remained to the present day.

Matthew sighed when they watched the boy disappear. "Poor lad," he said and swallowed hard. He took a deep breath. "Come. We must find the man."

The guard pointed out the direction, which went through the town and northwest toward the Sierra de Guadarama Mountains in the distance.

Philip broke in, "Did he have anything with him?"

The guard nodded. "*Si*, a large package, which he held under his arm."

Delgado had followed the main highway. Near midday he stopped at a tiny farmhouse and forced the family to give him food, draining their stores. They cursed the cardinal under their breath, but, of course, were unable to say or do a thing under threat of excommunication. They knew that it would be a lean year thanks to the man's greed.

Muttering a totally unconvincing, "May God bless you," accompanied by an even more unconvincing cross in the air, the big man walked on, munching the food almost continuously. Delgado turned up a track toward the mountain range looming high overhead. Later in the afternoon, puffing and wheezing with sweat pouring down his body, he came to a small hillock with a view of the hills beyond and a large smooth stone at its peak. Ideal. The wicked cardinal had packed all the items he would need and began to set up his evil altar right there. It took a while.

Matthew and Philip rode on through the forest for the better part of the day, checking all the paths leading off the highway. Eventually, as the sun approached the horizon, they came to the top of a rise and saw many more miles of forest laid out in front of them. Where else should they search? It seemed hopeless. The woods spread out for many miles on every side. Where could the man have gone?

Then came a quiet voice from the shadows of the trees. "Ah, *señor* priests, no doubt you have plenty of gold for a poor man."

The two men halted, thinking it had to be a robber. It was. A tall man rode from the shadows and stood before them. He raised a crossbow and aimed for Matthew. "All right, let's see what you have, then."

Matthew shook his head. "Nay, I am sorry, my man, but we have only a little food and no money at all."

"Really?" the robber sneered. "Then you will not mind my searching your load?"

Philip clenched his teeth. "*Señor*, could it not wait; we are on a very dangerous mission."

The robber laughed derisively. "My, my, my, the excuses I hear from some people. Nay, you can stay here until I have finished with you."

That was the last straw as far as Philip was concerned. The young friar spurred his horse forward. The bandit was not expecting resistance, especially from a holy man and his reaction was far too slow. Philip launched himself from his horse's back and leaped at the robber knocking him from his horse. The arrow went off, just missing Matthew's head and in the next second the robber was lying winded and disarmed. Philip didn't know how he had done it, but he was standing over the man's supine body, the point of his sword at the man's throat.

Matthew smiled in appreciation. "Well done, Philip. Your name?" he asked, looking at the bandit.

"Er … ah …" the bandit caught his breath and swallowed, "K … Kenda of Nadir."

Matthew nodded. "Very well, Kenda, you could possibly help us. We are, as we said before, on a dangerous mission to find a certain cardinal."

"Not Cardinal Delgado?" Kenda's face paled as he blurted out the question.

"The same. Have you seen him?"

For a few seconds, the robber hesitated—after all, there was a sharp point at his throat. "*Si*, he was heading out along this highway. I knew him and followed him for a while, but he had such a terrifying look on his face that I did not dare think about attacking him. He turned off the main road about a half-league ahead."

The two clerics grinned at each other. At last!

"Very well, *señor*," replied Matthew, "guide us. Now!"

Nodding and swallowing hard, Kenda stood, remounted his horse and rode ahead of them along the track that passed for a highway in those days. For a while they rode in silence, passing near the little farmhouse that Delgado had ransacked and when the sun touched the horizon, Kenda indicated a small track that turned off the road into the mountains. "That was the turnoff."

To back up his words, the two clerics saw a mutton bone, recently gnawed, lying on the ground a few feet up the track. This was indeed the path he had trod.

"After you," said Matthew meaningfully.

The robber repeated several words that would never be heard in polite company, which made the others blanch and led them down the track. In front of them they could see the first foothill looming up through the trees.

Meanwhile, as others had found before him, Delgado suddenly found the blasphemous text speaking itself. The evil cardinal was sweating hard as the tongue-twisting words flowed unbidden from his mouth.

"Delgado!" roared the voice of Azathoth. *"I know thee! I have known thee for these many years."*

Swallowing hard, the man addressed the empty air, "All right, you obviously know me. You know my power. I want more. Who are you and how can you help me?" Delgado wasn't sure, but … was there a slight tone of amusement in the next words?

"Thou only hast to say my name as thou crosses the threshold of The Great Door. The name thou must say is Azathoth."

The silver path and the great door appeared in front of the man.

"Come!" roared the voice of the spirit.

"No," cried a voice from behind Delgado and he turned. Matthew and Philip were approaching the hilltop, their faces masks of fear.

Kenda took one look at the apparition in front of him and fled in terror. A detached part of Matthew's mind thought wryly that it could be the start of many fireside tall tales.

Delgado looked at the two men and scowling furiously, he drew himself up to his full height. "What are you are doing here. You have no right to be here." He grabbed the battered crucifix from his belt and held it high. "Remove yourselves immediately, or you will find yourselves excommunicated and your souls dispatched to hell forever."

Matthew glanced at the altar and the path and door behind it and his eyes grew wide in horror. The cardinal had cast the very spell they had been talking about. His fear of the unknown evil overcame his fear of excommunication. He drew his own crucifix and held it high as he shouted, "My Lord Cardinal, powerful, as you are, you do not have the power to hold or control such evil."

But Delgado smiled mirthlessly at the young priest. "I have—and I will have even more," he wheezed. Since the two priests showed no sign of leaving, he flung his head back, let the crucifix fall to swing at his belt and laughed as his long, greasy hair flailed in the air.

"Very well, my priests, stand there; watch and understand the meaning of true and unlimited power and then prepare to be obliterated."

"No, my Lord," shouted the other, his terror rising by the second. "Such power as you see before you is not for any human man—Christian or heathen. You cannot take it without giving up your soul in exchange. I beg you, *señor*, come back."

Delgado scoffed at the two men then turned, his greed for power blinding him to what horror there could be.

The voice of Azathoth roared louder than ever.

"Come! Come! The power over all is yours!"

The two priests, hearing the monster's voice coming from the empty air, stood frozen with fear. With trembling hands, Matthew held up a consecrated wafer, but it only elicited a horrible laugh from the disembodied voice.

"Thy pitiful attempt to overcome my powers is totally useless!"

Matthew gasped. This was the Body of Christ that the evil spirit was spurning. "You must bow to the power from the altar," he cried.

But the voice only laughed harder.

"Ye think that a piece of thin bread, a floury wafer, can stop my power. Ye have much to learn about the power of Azathoth."

The wafer exploded into powder in the young man's hand. Matthew felt tears of despair fill his eyes as his beliefs evaporated. It seemed that nothing could stop Delgado from opening the Door to Hell. The wicked cardinal had reached the door, seeming not to have heard the exchange and wheezing and sweating, opened his mouth to pronounce the blasphemous name. Both priests prepared themselves for oblivion.

Utter desperation prompted Philip to offer one of the simplest prayers of all: "Lord God, help us." He had never meant a prayer more in his life.

It might have been a tiny prayer but the effect could not have been more dramatic. Azathoth began roaring again as the monster's power was ripped away. Unaware that the monster's power was being decimated, Matthew—thinking their situation desperate and almost hopeless—did the only thing he could think of: he began to pray the Lord's Prayer under his breath.

Over the roar, Delgado shouted grandly and almost formally in tones of victory, unaware of what was taking place. "I have called thee according to the wording of *The Necronomicon*. Thou hast answered my call. Now fulfil thy promise. *Azathoth*!"

The door burst open and a huge claw smashed down. A guillotine could not have been more effective. The evil cardinal stood there silently, a look of pained surprise on his face. Then his disgustingly fat, bloated body fell apart in two halves, spurting blood, gore, liquid fat and worse in every direction and as it hit the ground it vanished in a cloud of oily, evil-smelling smoke.

The two men stood there, Matthew's Paternoster's closing words fading, the amen no more than a whisper. Both clerics were trembling violently in sheer terror as they waited.

A light surrounded the Door of Hell and the door and path suddenly disappeared. There was a deathly silence for several seconds as the light formed into a cool, gently shining circle. Then the two clerics heard a different voice from the light, a still small voice that seemed to echo all around and give the impression of greatly understated but unlimited power.

"Well done, my son. Your faith has foiled the evil one."

"Who … who are you?" came Matthew's frightened whisper as both men collapsed to their knees.

"I am … that I am," came the reply, causing them both to gasp as they recognised the fabulous, well-known words that God had used to identify himself to Moses in the Old Testament. (The Hebrew name YHVH—pronounced Yahweh—that Jews know as the Name of God is so revered that they don't dare *say* it. Christians pronounce it Jehovah, which translates to I am.)

The voice continued quietly, "Just as Azathoth came when summoned, so do I. But you do not need complicated incantations and strange implements: just a simple prayer."

Philip shook his head in bewilderment. "My Lord, surely you mock me. How could my simple prayer summon **you**?" The last word was spoken with the uttermost awe. The young friar was stunned. At that moment he was suddenly very aware of how immeasurably small he was and how unutterably huge the great Yahweh was.

Matthew dared to think there was almost a light, happy sound to the next words as if the speaker were smiling.

"I made the law long ago that I would always come when summoned in faith, even by a child's bedside prayer. Do you think that I would not obey my own laws? Remember, I am with you always even unto the end of the world. Go now in peace. My blessing will be upon you and those you deal with for the rest of your days."

The last few words sounded like a trumpet call. Then there was silence again. The two men rose trembling, looking at each other and shaking their heads, unable to take in what had just happened. Then Matthew put his arms around the younger man.

"My brother, all is well. Thanks to your faith the world is safe from that terrible monster."

The tears stood in Philip's eyes and he felt as though his heart would burst. They had spoken with the Infinite. Both were aware that their lives would never be the same again.

After they had finally calmed down, Matthew walked over to where Delgado had stood and bending down, picked up the translated copy of *The Necronomicon* that they had worked on so hard and for so long. "He'll not need this again and neither will we."

The two men made their way off into the darkness. When they came to a clifftop, they looked down and could see the glitter of a stream at the bottom of a deep ravine some four hundred feet below. Philip cast the black book into the darkness and they both heard it meet the bottom far below with a quiet *floppity-splash*. *It would*, thought Philip, *be destroyed eventually by the elements and the ravine was so deep nobody could get to it.*

When they turned away, they did not notice a strange but familiar shadow detach itself from the surrounding darkness, pick up the book and make its way to a cave nearby. The two men bade farewell to each other on the final journey and went back to their parishes.

Philip went on to take Holy Orders and devoted his life not to eternal prayer as most priests did, but to helping others. After a few years he became assistant priest to his vicar and then when the old man died, Philip became archdeacon to the seven churches of his parish and served them well until his death some thirty-six years later. When he passed on, he was sadly missed by all.

Matthew returned to his parish in Ubeda. In later years people said that his sermons once full of hellfire, brimstone and damnation were now full of light and love and happiness. The people grew to love not only his sermons, but also to love and respect each other. Until the end of his days, Father Matthew's parish was the happiest in Spain.

Eventually the Inquisition came to an end and its implements were cast away. The great castle of the Inquisition swiftly fell into ruins.

It was rumoured that if any came near the place in the Spanish mountains where the evil altar had been prepared and listened carefully, they might just hear the sound of screaming, which some said was the soul of a totally unrepentant wicked cardinal, who now suffered through all eternity for the memory of the towering evil he had done to so many others.

In the deepest vault of the castle in the dirt floor under one particular flagstone, lay a box sealed with tallow. Inside lay a familiar old scroll, manuscripted in ancient Arabic on parchment and bound with three leather thongs.

In a niche in a dry, cool cave deep in an unknown valley some miles outside Madrid, lay a roughly bound book in Medieval Latin—waiting.

Both waited for the day when they would be discovered—the day that would once again bring to light … *The Necronomicon*.

Chapter Six

AD 1549
Madrid, Spain

Dr. John Dee, astrologer and mathematician to Queen Elizabeth I of England—on a fact-finding tour of Spain—looked down into the large hole in the floor of the ruin.

"So what is it?" he asked, turning to the Spanish guide.

"Well, this whole building used to be the Castle of the Inquisition, *señor*," answered Lopez, bowing slightly. "So this would be the entrance to the dungeons. It looks very dangerous."

Lopez was a little in awe of this man who had come into his life so precipitously and who was paying him more money than Lopez had ever seen in his life, simply to show him around.

Dee put his foot onto the wooden floor. It sagged suddenly under the slight pressure. "*Hmm*, you could be right," he replied, removing his foot quickly.

"Do you want to see down into it?" asked Lopez, biting his tongue as he said it, hoping the man would object. In this he was doomed to disappointment.

"I do," replied Dee shortly. "I want to know all there is about the area. I have studied the Inquisition and I want to know all about the places it operated from and how it performed its tasks." Dee's eyes looked into the distance. "More to the point, I want to find out why it was so evil."

He turned to the other man accompanying him, a surly young

fellow. "What say you, Johann? Should we go in? I dearly want to look around and possibly learn something about this castle."

Johann pursed his lips. "I could not say, *señor*," he replied hesitantly. "It does indeed look dangerous."

Dee nodded. "Tell me," he continued, turning to Lopez, "are there any other people near here who know about this place?"

Lopez thought. "I think there is a hermit who lives nearby who may know a lot about the castle that others do not."

"Good. Johann, go and find him if you would and we will question him."

"Where will I find you?" asked Johann.

"We shall return to Madrid. We will be staying in the good Dr. Krueger's house. You may seek us there."

Johann nodded, tuned and went off to the east.

* * *

"Yes? What do you want?" creaked a voice from the depths of a cave.

Johann swallowed hard and took his courage with both hands. "*Señor*, I have come to speak to you on behalf of *Señor* John Dee, who wishes to know about the Castle of the Inquisition. Can you tell him anything about it?"

There was a chuckle from the cave and then the darkness seemed to form itself into a man. The figure came out and stood there staring at Johann, who felt more and more vulnerable. The man looked relatively young but had the oldest eyes Johann had ever seen.

Finally the figure spoke, "Dee, *eh*? Yes, I know of the man. What would he want with the Inquisition?"

Johann licked his lips. "Dr. Dee has come over to study the Inquisition," he ventured, his heart beating wildly, "and to write ... I think he called it a 'tree-tise' about it when he goes back to England."

"I see."

"So any information you can give us would be very useful."

The figure nodded again. "Very well, I will come to his dwelling."

Johann informed the man where Dee was staying and—just as this worthy was turning away—said, "*Señor*, what name shall I give?"

"Ah … yes … my name." The man looked a little hesitant, then continued, "Well, I have rarely used a name, but since you need it, the name is Muerte: Petro Muerte."

The name meant nothing to Johann. He nodded, took his leave swiftly and returned to Madrid.

The information was eventually passed on and Dee readied himself for the meeting.

* * *

"Herr Doctor?"

"Yes, my man?" Dr. Dee put down his pen as Dr. Krueger stood respectfully at the door.

"It's a man called Petro. He wishes to speak with you."

"Ah yes, Johann told me about him. Show him in."

"Herr Doctor, I think I should mention … er …" The little German doctor looked uncomfortable. "He's not a very nice man."

Dee gave a slight smile. "That is perfectly all right. Show him in with great haste."

"This way, Mein Herr," said Krueger, turning to the figure that now stood behind him.

He was answered with a growl. Then Petro Muerte stepped into the room and stood looking around. Dee found himself thinking that the man looked like a dog sampling the air in a strange place.

"*Señor* Doctor Dee?" The voice seemed to creak from a great distance.

"I am he," replied Dee, "and I understand you know something of the Castle of the Inquisition?"

The man gave a snort. "Indeed I do, *Señor* Dee. How much would you be wanting to know?"

Dee motioned Muerte to a large comfortable seat and reached for a fresh parchment. "I want to know all about it—as much as you know, Petro. You must tell me."

The man nodded and sat for a minute or so thinking and then said, "All right, how much of the Spanish Inquisition do you know?"

Dee smiled wryly. "Not very much: only as much as the gypsies and tinkers and troubadours tell on their rounds. Their stories are graphic enough to give children nightmares, but it would seem that there is far more to it than they know."

Muerte nodded. "Indeed there is, *señor* and if you have about a week, I will tell you all you need to know."

Dee rubbed his hands together in delight. *At last, here is someone who actually knows about the accursed Inquisition and is willing to talk.*

"In that case, you must start from the beginning and tell me all." The man's eyes grew wide with anticipation. "And in as much detail as you can. I want to know it all."

Muerte raised his hand. "Before you begin, *señor*, I wish to know something of you as well. I understand you have had dealings with the occult. Perhaps a little magic?"

Dee raised his eyebrows. Now how on earth had this man known that? He pursed his lips, then replied, "I have only studied it from afar, but I have never actually done any magic myself. I leave that to the people who are able to do so. I count myself only a learner, not a doer."

Muerte nodded. He had thought as much. "Then, *señor*, you are familiar with the wording of old books. I can use that to better describe my tale."

He settled himself deep into the upholstery and closed his eyes, marshalling his thoughts.

Dee dipped a freshly sharpened goose quill and licked his lips. The knowledge he had sought was just around the corner. The doctor waited expectantly.

When Muerte began to speak, his voice might have been deemed boring if Dee had not been so interested, but the doctor wrote, questioned, listened and wrote again.

It took only four days—not the week—to tell all that Muerte knew and by then Dee had filled more than sixty sheets of parchment with his small neat copperplate writing.

And what there was to tell. Several times Dee found himself wondering if Muerte had possibly had dealings with the Inquisition himself after some facts came out that only an inquisitor could have known. However, Muerte followed each of these up with the trite statement, "Of course, this was information which was passed on to me by a renegade priest." Dee was willing to take that at face value.

They spoke and wrote far into the nights, pausing only when they ran out of candles. Muerte slept on the floor alongside the fire and in the days that followed, they began again after Kruger's servants served them a good breakfast.

After four days, Muerte finally said, "And that, *Señor* Doctor, is all I know." The man seemed to hesitate, then raised a finger. "One more point. I am led to understand that the last Grand Inquisitor, a Cardinal named Delgado, came upon a book of great power that he used very selfishly and it brought him to a very sticky end."

Dee pricked up his ears. "A book? Which book?"

Muerte's lips twitched before being replaced by his normally solemn expression. "I don't know if you would be interested."

"I would," retorted the doctor shortly. "I told you, *señor*—everything you know."

Muerte nodded. "Very well, *señor*, the scroll was reputed to be ..." The man paused for effect, then, with his eyes deliberately boring into the other, he said, "*The Necronomicon.*"

There was dead silence as Dee looked at the other and swallowed hard. In all his life, he had only once before heard about the fabulous *Necronomicon* from an old wizard who had lived in the backcountry of Summerset and he had made up his mind that if it existed, he would find it. Now this man was pronouncing the name as if it actually did exist.

"B … but …" Dee stumbled, then decided to play devil's advocate to see what would happen. "But *The Necronomicon* does not exist," he replied forcefully. "I have heard that it is only a fable."

Muerte grinned wryly. "That is what the church would wish you to believe. In fact, it does exist and I have every reason to believe that there may be a copy hidden somewhere in the ruins …"—he looked pointedly at the wall, behind which in the distance lay the ruins of the Inquisition—"of the castle."

Dee went pale. A copy of *The Necronomicon* actually at hand. Incredible!

"Are you sure?" he finally managed to croak out.

Muerte nodded.

Dee swallowed again. "Then I must search for it as soon as possible." The man had forgotten that Muerte was there, as he began to make his plans.

"*Señor.*"

Dee looked up. "Oh yes, Petro," he added absently, "I thank thee very much for your information. You will be well paid," and he reached for his purse.

Muerte grinned. "Not needed, *Señor* Dee." The man smiled and waved the purse of gold away. "I am only too pleased to be of help to anyone who needs it." The creaking voice gave a chuckle. "I wish you godspeed, *señor* and may your exploration be fruitful."

"I thank you." Dee nodded as the man went out the door and was engrossed in his notes before that worthy had passed out of sight.

* * *

Muerte came out of the house, nodded to the doorman and with a very crafty look turned his face back to his cave in the hills. The seed was sown. Now, let the good doctor—Muerte gave an evil chuckle as his mind repeated the word *good*—search until he found the scroll. Then … maybe …

Muerte chuckled again.

* * *

A week or so later, Dee and his two companions, Lopez and Johaan and a small crowd of carpenters made their way into the ruins of the Castle of the Inquisition and carefully made their way down through the dank, crumbling, echoing corridors. They moved with extreme care, for there was danger in every step. The man in front had a large axe and tapped the wood and stone floors as they progressed. In two hours, they had advanced no more than fifty yards. A door appeared around a corner, originally barred and locked, but now rotted and hanging on one hinge. Again, the floor sagged under the men's feet as they progressed.

"Place a bridge," commanded Dee, "and let us see what may be found."

The man next to him reached into his bag and drew out a number of short planks of stout wood. These were carefully placed and the men entered the room. Inside were the remains of a rotting quill and a wooden inkwell on the table and two wooden candlesticks on the windowsill; otherwise, the room was bare. Little did they know they were looking at the scene that saw the translation of *The Necronomicon*. The two men who did the deed, however, had long since gone to their maker.

After a short but thorough examination of the room, Dee left for other places. Although there were other offices, all books, parchments and other regalia of the Inquisition had long since disappeared. The men faced bare rooms, several of which had lost their ceilings and were open to the sky.

"No birds," muttered one of the carpenters.

"*Hmm?*" Dee raised his eyebrows.

"No birds," repeated the man. "There should be birds nesting in a place like this, but there are no birds anywhere. Not even bird droppings."

Dee squared his jaw and swallowed. The man was quite right. Even the ubiquitous sparrow was missing. Dee knew that birds were very sensitive to evil and if they had all forsaken a place then said place must be far from wholesome. Swallowing hard, he crossed himself.

They slowly progressed through passageways and stairwells until they finally arrived at what had once been the torture chamber. They were able to make much faster progress now as the floor was stone. The huge wooden door flew to bits under the hammer blows of the carpenters and the explorers entered. After a swift glance around, Dee nodded with a grim, mirthless smile. This was the centre of the Inquisition's "The Question, Both Ordinary and Extraordinary."

The man shuddered as he thought of the horrors that had been perpetrated in this dreadful room of despair. There up against the far wall, now partially covered in a slimy verdigris, was the huge throne of the inquisitor, who had overseen the terrors and agonies inflicted by his priests. They saw the rack, the iron maiden, the thumbscrew and the rusting remains of the brazier for heating the irons to red-white heat, which then was pressed into living flesh. At various places around the dungeon—like some unholy Stations of the Cross—lay the remains of other items of torture, their uses Dee could not fathom. The man swallowed hard and looked around, shaking his head in sorrow. How could men—priests yet—cause such evil to others?

The small band made their way farther into the rabbit warren of tunnels that led deeper and deeper into the earth. Each layer of dungeons was explored carefully. They found several skeletal remains and Dee, as a fully registered priest, sorrowfully pronounced a benediction over each one. Then he drew a map of each room in the layer and its place in the castle was carefully noted.

Day followed day. The men had been whittled down to Lopez and Johann, who were both strong and could endure the stomach-turning smells they encountered so often. The two followed Dee from room to room, assisting where they were needed and carefully searching the floors and walls for secret openings as required.

Dee inspected the whole castle from top to bottom. Although little was gained from their inspection, he was able to tie in the various rooms and their contents, such as they were, with the information already given to him by Muerte.

Four days later, Dee and his friends reached the very bottom of the dungeons, the *oubliette*. There was no room deeper and Dee was starting to think that Muerte must have been mistaken: there was no copy of *The Necronomicon* that he could find.

Without any prompting, the two men started on their job of exploring. Johann began tapping the walls and inserting his knife into the cracks of the stone, while Lopez began turning over the lose flagstones of the dungeon. The flickering light of the lantern cast an eerie pall over the scene as Dee looked hard at the walls while Johann worked. The usual rusty leg and arm irons hung from the eyelets in the wall and on one side lay a rusty blade, which looked like a scythe blade but was so rusty and corroded that it was more hole than blade. Dee pursed his lips as he tried to think of how it had been used, but he finally had to admit defeat. The only people who could have told him were long since dust.

Suddenly, Lopez's knife hit a certain flagstone rock. "*Señor* Dee, I think I may have found something," he cried and as the other two came running, the man proceeded to carefully lift out the stone and unearth the box underneath. It was about two feet long, wrapped in oilcloth and carefully sealed.

Dee was almost beside himself with excitement. "I thank thee," he cried and relieved Lopez of his burden.

"But *Señor* Dee," cried the man, anxiety giving his tongue an unusual freedom, "do I not get paid?"

Dee burst out laughing." Of course, my friend, of course. You have given me quite a treasure here. Come, follow me."

Dee left hurriedly, the two men jogging after him. Arriving back above ground, he reached into his purse and gave the two men twenty gold pieces each (the equivalent value of a twenty-first century, four-bedroomed house). The men were staggered. This was more money than each had ever hoped to see in his lifetime. They stumbled backwards, pulling their forelocks, then turned and bolted in case Dee asked for the money back. Dee, however, had eyes only for the packet. He quickly took it back to his room at Dr. Krueger's and set it on the table. Carefully, he broke the tallow seal, which he now noted was the seal of the Inquisition: a cross surmounting a crossed sword and scroll. Nodding sagely, he unwrapped the oilcloth, revealing a sealed box. He broke the seal and opened the lid. Inside was a smaller cylindrical packet, wrapped in more oilcloth and from it he drew out a singular item—a thick, ancient, parchment scroll bound with leather thongs.

Carefully, his heart thundering against his ribs, Dee unrolled the scroll to the first page and saw the sprawling Arabic title. He clenched his jaw trying to recall his minuscule knowledge of Arabic as he tried to translate the first three words. Eventually it came … "Song of Demons," he muttered, his face pale. "*Demon Song*. In the name of God Almighty, it **is** *The Necronomicon*."

Dee sat down quickly, his heart in his mouth. The Inquisition treatise was forgotten. He was now privy to one of the most fabulous and terrifying books in the whole world. Now he must find out what evil was contained in this incredible book. He'd heard so many rumors and now it would be good to know the truth after all this. After some thought, he decided that it must be removed and taken back to England. There he could work on it in safety—*yes, in safety,* his mind repeated.

Somewhere, something evil sniggered.

* * *

Her Majesty Queen Elizabeth, the first of that name and Queen of England and Ireland, was speaking to her astrologer, but their conversation was not about astrology.

"Dr. Dee, sir, I have not seen you for many a day. What wouldst you all this time?"

Dee smiled as he dofted his hat with a typically Elizabethan flourish and bowed to his sovereign. "Ma'am, 'tis a singular job I am performing at this time. I was recently in Spain …"

"Yes, I thought it might have something to do with that," interrupted Elizabeth, nodding.

Dee nodded. "Yes and I have found a literary treasure the likes of which no one could have guessed. I am working on the translation of this scroll now. It is very time consuming, for the language is archaic Arabic and I have much to learn about the language before I can write the full copy. I am using all the resources from Oxford and Cambridge Universities, as well as several people who have knowledge of these things."

Elizabeth nodded, her lace ruff bobbing at the movement. "Thank you, good doctor, I will want a full report when you are finished." The great woman gave a wry grin. "Take your time and get it right."

Dee smiled broadly. "I will indeed, Your Majesty."

Elizabeth's smile became more businesslike. "Good. Now, about this meeting with the French ambassador in two weeks' time; what approach do the stars suggest I take with this man?"

* * *

Doctor Dee continued to translate the scroll but it was slow going. As he told the Queen, the language was so far out of date as to be almost incomprehensible, but gradually he was able to work it out. Slowly, over several years, he wrote the full script of *The Necronomicon*. He did a number of tours in this time to Poland and Bohemia, but always not far from his mind was the manuscript of the fabulous book.

One evening he paid a visit to the Queen.

"Your Majesty, I have some of the book translated. It is an incredible book."

"What is this book called?" asked Elizabeth.

"It's called *The Necronomicon—The Book of Dead Names*. The original name is *Al Azif*, which appears to be a Sumerian phrase that could only be translated as Demon Song. The name describes the noises in the night made by insects, which in ancient times was thought to be the whispering of demons. It seems to be a magical book, detailing a number of very powerful magical spells."

Elizabeth pursed her lips. "It sounds dangerous."

Dee nodded. "Yes, it could be, but only to those who attempt to cast the spells. I certainly do not intend to try." The doctor blew out his cheeks. "That would be inviting disaster."

Elizabeth nodded. "Very good, my doctor. Keep going."

Dee nodded and bowed as he left.

* * *

Dee returned home and since it was not too late, he decided that he would work on one last spell before retiring. He sat at his desk, looked at the title and wrote:

A Spelle for the Closing of an Portale of Evil

Imagine a ringe of irone around thee heade and an booke bounde with fur in thee handes ...

After Dee carefully translated the spell, something—Dee knew not what—prompted him to commit the spell to memory. He went over it. It was a comparatively simple spell, in which he had to imagine a band of iron around his head and a fur-bound book open in front of him. That was easy. He continued to learn the spell, which required saying a seven-syllable word and drawing a certain shape in midair. Dee kept the spell in mind and went over it again before lying down to sleep that night.

* * *

"The Honourable Doctor John Dee, Royal Astrologer," came the footman's loud voice and Dee entered the ballroom of the large mansion.

It was the domicile of the great writer Sir Francis Bacon and he was having an "at home," to which all the great names of the period were invited.

"Dee, my dear fellow," boomed Bacon's voice as the large man walked over to the astrologer. Dee smiled and the two shook hands. "Still working on the stuffy old book?"

Dee's work was common knowledge although the contents were not. One rumour said it was a scroll from Egypt full of evil pagan rituals, though how that got around not even Dee knew.

"Yes, Sir Francis, I am indeed—and finding it very hard work."

"Ah well, keep on. You'll get it right I am sure." Bacon was far more interested in the doings of the Queen and he went on to question Dee in great detail.

As the evening wore on, the dances were announced and the little band of two treble viols[2], a tenor viol, a lute, an oboe, an alto sackbut[3] and a tambourine, broke into a set of the latest courantes and galliards. The pairs style of dancing had become quite fashionable in recent years and now a number of the current composers had taken peasant dances and adapted them for the aristocracy's "at-homes." The guests were informed that several of the quaint

---

[2] This instrument was the forerunner of the violin and other strings.

[3] This was a slide-brass, available in all sizes and eventually developed into the trombone.

tunes had been arranged by a hitherto unknown young German Clergyman and Composer named Jakob Obrecht. After listening to them for a while, Dee shook his head, firmly convinced that the man's works would swiftly pass into obscurity and oblivion.

Dee himself took no part in the dances; he was not a dancer and without any sense of rhythm whatsoever would never be. The phrase *two left feet* had, he was sure, been invented especially for him. He sat at a table with a glass of fine Madera at his elbow and watched the slow and gentle gyrations of the dancers—a pretty display, but not really to his liking. He longed to be back with *The Necronomicon*.

Seated on his right, two tables away, was a solemn and thoughtful young man who occasionally wrote on a parchment.

"Who is that?" asked Dee to a passing footman.

"Sir, that is Mr. William Shakespeare. He has just begun as a playwright. Indeed, I have spoken to several actors and they say that he has shown some considerable talent."

Dee nodded cynically. "Has he written anything of worth yet?"

"Indeed a play of his was produced only two months ago and was well received by the *Populousque Londonus*[4]. You might have heard of it: *Comedy of Errors*. I understand he is working on another, a historical play, but other than that I do not know. I'll definitely be going to see it."

Dee shook his head. *Hmmph, another one-day-wonder*, he thought cynically.[5]

"Doctor Dee?" The voice came from his left.

Dee looked around and saw a young man dressed in the height of fashion, a glass of port in one hand, a pomander in the other and both little fingers raised in the air. Dee's mind did a quick scan. Robert Devereaux, soon to be second lord of Essex, another

---

[4] Pig-Latin for 'The People of London'

[5] Which just goes to show how wrong one can be.

favourite of the Queen.

Dee bowed from the chair. "Mr. Devereaux."

"May I join you, sir?"

The doctor nodded to the chair next to him.

Devereaux sat down and Dee nodded toward the bard. "Have you actually seen any of that man's plays? I understand he is a playwright of some repute, but I have had no time to contemplate taking in a play and less of seeing one."

Devereaux smiled. "I, too, have had little time to visit his specialised theatre. It is called The Globe. Apparently he is working on a historical play, *Henry VI*. I don't know how it is going to end, but it sounds good."

Dee chuckled. "Will never last," he grunted. "I'll give that man a year. After that, he will never be heard of again."

Then they both paused as the footman stepped forward and addressed the crowd. "Gentlemen, pray take your partners for a new form of the Pavane." The band struck up the slow, stately rhythm.

For a moment, they both watched the dancers.

"You are not dancing?" asked Devereaux.

"Sir, I do not dance." Dee was short. He felt it was no one's business but his own.

The young man nodded. "I am afraid that we differ. I love it, but I have no partner this evening and all the ladies had their cards filled early."

They continued to make polite conversation as the evening went on and, strangely enough, Dee found himself beginning to like the man. Devereaux himself was warming to this otherwise austere man, who could carry on a very interesting conversation.

Eventually the evening came to a close. After a final rousing tordion and allemande, which had all the dancers panting and laughing, the orchestra packed their instruments and departed and Dee and Devereaux, both a little in their cups, thanked their host warmly.

Bacon smiled as the two stumbled out into the darkness to their Hansom cabs.

Little did he know what this meeting would give rise to.

* * *

"Is Doctor Dee within?" asked Devereaux, from the step.

"Aye sir," replied Henry Oates, Dee's Cornish butler. "Oi'll just tell him thou'rt here. Would loike to wait in t' library?" He showed the young man to a room lined with books.

Devereaux looked around the library at the vast collection of books that Dee had collected. Very wide reaching, he observed with topics, ranging from pure mathematical applications to astrology. Dee was quite a scholar.

"Devereaux, my dear fellow," came Dee's voice as he entered and the two shook hands.

Devereaux smiled. "I thought to continue the talk we began the other night at Bacon's 'at home.' I enjoyed it so much."

Dee smiled wider, flattered at such a compliment. "Thank you, sir. You are most kind. Actually I was working at a translation. I have been working at it for some time now. Would you like to see it?"

Devereaux nodded and the doctor led the way to a workroom piled high on all sides with books of all colours and sizes, many dripping bookmarks. On a large table in the middle of the room was a strange and very ancient parchment scroll, opened about halfway through. Alongside it was a pile of paper, the top sheet of which had writing halfway down the page.

Dee smiled and said with the pride of a father, "My masterwork."

Devereaux's eyebrows raised. He was impressed. The young man walked over to the table and quickly read down the page.

A Spelle to Finde Jeweles Where None May Be Seen

"Ah, so the rumours were true—it is a spell book," said the man.

Dee nodded. "Yes, it is and a more powerful spell book I have yet to see. But I feel that it should not be used, for the spells seem strange, almost as if they were disguised. Some are ..." and the doctor grinned, "badly out of date. We know so much more now than the writer of the original did then and one or two of the spells are easily explainable by common sense. However ..." and the learned man paused, a finger raised.

Devereaux looked at him, his eyes wide in anticipation.

Pursing his lips, Dee continued, "There is one spell which quite frankly is terrifying. It is this one."

The man turned the pages of his translation back until he uncovered one particular page and Devereaux swallowed when he read the title:

Ye Counjuration of the Openinge of ye Door to All Power, Knowledge and Enlightenmente

Looking over the man's shoulder, Dee said, "I feel that nobody should be allowed to use such a spell. Ordinary folk such as us could not hope to control such power if it were unleashed."

Devereaux's face was solemn as he nodded, but his mind was turning cartwheels. *What power the spell must control*, he thought. In that moment, Robert Devereaux's greed took over and he decided that whatever happened, he would get that spell and cast it for himself.

* * *

In the late summer of 1594, a certain ceremony took place.

"Arise, Robert Devereaux, second Lord of Essex," proclaimed Elizabeth and the young man rose from his genuflect, desperately trying to keep his face straight while exalting inside. He now was privy to the title, estates and huge income of the Duchy of Essex, one of the richest in the kingdom and he was well pleased.

The courtiers applauded dutifully and Devereaux turned to Dee who was standing nearby. "Sir, I would like to invite you to join

Her Majesty and myself in the house for a Madera."

Dee smiled widely. "Sir, I would be very glad to accept."

Elizabeth smiled as her two favourites spoke. "Very well, my nobles, I will gladly join you both for drinks."

Smiling, she moved toward the door accompanied by the two men. As they walked, Devereaux gave a meaningful glance at a black-clad figure standing alongside the door: the Queen's physician, Rodrigo Lopez. The Spaniard watched the two exit and smiled to himself.

* * *

Later two shadows met in the dark streets in the more down-at-heel part of London. "Hast the bottle?" asked one to the other.

"I have," replied the other and a small phial changed hands.

The receiver turned and hurried away into the darkness.

Devereaux smiled to himself, a smile completely without humour, as he watched the Spaniard disappear. Now the trap was set, but not for the Queen. The trap was set for Lopez, the Queen's doctor and Devereaux's stepping-stone to Elizabeth's good books. If he timed it right, he would be even more in the Queen's favour and would also stand to gain considerable titles.

* * *

"Your Majesty," cried Devereaux, hurrying into the throne room and rushing to the throne, "please, I must speak with you now."

Elizabeth looked up in surprise as her favourite flung himself onto one knee in front of her.

"M'Lord Essex, what is the meaning of this?"

"Your Majesty," cried the young man, seemingly in anguish, "there is a plot against your person."

Elizabeth's eyes grew wide. "How did you come by such a piece of information?"

Devereaux stood, his face a picture of concern. "I overheard a conversation this past night as I was passing Tower Bridge on the way home. It appeared to concern a bottle of Hemlock, which was to be applied either to your food or to your medicine."

Elizabeth was in the habit of taking various potions prescribed by her doctor and her face turned pale. "Hemlock! Essex, if this is right, then you must go through the belongings of anyone who has been close to me for the last night. The person found with the poison is to be tried and executed for treason. Could you identify the persons involved?"

Essex looked troubled. "I could only see one man's face and that by the somewhat uncertain light of the moon. However, it did indeed look somewhat like your physician, Rodrigo Lopez."

The Queen's jaw dropped. Then her usually gentle contralto became a shrieking soprano as she issued a string of orders. In a moment, a platoon of household cavalry guards were rushing to Lopez's quarters.

Behind his mask of concern, Essex wore an evil smile as the armed men hurried passed him. The first part of his plan was up and running.

* * *

The palace guards entered Lopez's room and with no more than the usual difficulty, they went through all the doctor's goods. Of course, it was quite in the cards for the doctor to have some poisons on his person—after all he was a doctor and poisons were part of his trade, but the guards were looking for a particular poison. Although they were all illiterate, they had been given shingles with the name scrawled in charcoal. They looked at the labels of the various bottles and phials and soon found what they were looking for.

"Here be the bottle," called the young guard as he held up a small bottle with a glass stopper and gave it to his commander along with his shingle. The older man could clearly read the Latin word, *Haemlokus*. He nodded, his lips clenched—Hemlock.

***

A stunned Rodrigo Lopez stood between two guards. The incriminating bottle that he had gotten from Devereaux contained ordinary Thames water, but that would never come to light. It stood on the table; Exhibit A.

Most folk knew that Hemlock had no other purpose except for poisoning an enemy.

"B … but, Your Majesty, that drug is for my studies. It is not for any other use."

"Where did you obtain the bottle?"

"Er … er … er …" Lopez was stumped. He hadn't quite gotten that far in his made-up story. Hemlock was almost impossible to obtain in England. Finally, he said the first name that came to mind: "Sweden."

"Rubbish. Sweden does not produce Hemlock." The Queen's voice was almost conversational.

Lopez had made plans with Devereaux to murder the Queen so that Devereaux could become king and Lopez his prime minister. They planned to rule the world.

Lopez saw Devereaux enter. There was a slight sneer on the young man's face when he saw his fellow conspirator in chains. The second part of his plan was working very well.

"Y … Your Majesty," cried Lopez, grasping at the straw this offered, "there is your traitor. That man there," and he pointed at Devereaux.

Devereaux's mouth fell open and his face was a mask of indignation as he said, "Traitor? How dare you, sir. Your Majesty, I will not even honour that accusation with an answer. Will you believe a commoner over the sworn word of a nobleman? I know I am innocent of such a heinous crime."

Elizabeth sat there looking from one to the other. She was likely to believe Devereaux, but Lopez looked sincere. What to do?

Finally she decided to give her favourite the benefit of the doubt. After all, she had just proclaimed him Lord of Essex. Surely he would not want to murder her: no, definitely not.

"Rodrigo Lopez, it is the finding of our court that you are guilty. You shall be taken from here to the tower and there your head shall be removed from your body as a punishment for the crime of high treason to our person. And may God have mercy on your soul."

Devereaux could not resist a tiny smile of triumph as Lopez was dragged away screaming. When he again turned to the Queen, his face showed innocent indignation as he shook his head. "Why should one be so evil," he said. "Your Majesty is right to deal with him so."

Elizabeth nodded, but something niggled at her. She decided to keep her eye on the young man as he bowed his way out of the room.

Two days later Lopez was dragged into the execution square and beheaded. Just before the axe fell he snarled at the sky. "Curse you, Devereaux, curse you to hell."

The axe fell and Lopez was no more.

* * *

Michael MacDonell and Patrick O'Shea were addressing the crowd before them. Sometime in the future, their company would be known as the IRA, but presently they were simply known as Irish rebels.

"The Orangemen have overstepped the mark once too often," screamed O'Shea indignantly, "and it is up to us to put a stop to their evil ways. May St. Patrick and the Blessed Virgin be with us as we go on this honourable and holy crusade against them."

The crowd roared its approval. Armed and dangerous and Catholics to a man, they were far-right activators. The two leaders had built up to this moment and after a few more screamed implications, they led the ragtag army out into the sunlight and into war.

* * *

Elizabeth gaped. There was an uprising in Londonderry. Even as she read the message that had been delivered by a panting messenger, she was aware that battles were raging in the little city between Orangemen and Catholics. Shaking her head in sadness, she called her advisors and put the problem to them.

It was the prime minister who finally recommended that she send a small army and put down the rebellion.

"But who should I send as a commander?" asked the great woman.

Doctor Dee, standing in the background, took it all in and bethought himself of his friend. Devereaux had spoken to him many times about the battles he had fought in times past and it did not enter Dee's head that the man could possibly be boasting. He spoke up for the first time.

"Ma'am, I would seriously suggest you use Devereaux, Lord Essex. He tells me that he has had considerable experience in this sort of thing. Allow him to lead the army and the rebellion will soon be crushed."

Elizabeth nodded. She knew how close Dee and Devereaux had become in the past few years.

"Very well, Doctor, I will accept your recommendation. Send word to Lord Essex that I command him to take an army and put down the rebellion in Londonderry."

A messenger left within a half-hour to travel the road to Essex and deliver the message.

* * *

Devereaux swallowed hard as his army began its task in the streets of Londonderry. Under it all, in spite of all the campaigns he had fought, he was a coward and had no stomach for this sort of thing. Right now he was regretting the boasting lies he had told his friend.

He found it safer to lead the army from the back as he had always done, but by the time they got there, the uprising appeared to be over—the Catholics had won and all was quiet again. For several hours the army patrolled the streets, but they found nothing. However, just as Devereaux was breathing a sigh of relief and framing the words in his mind to command a return to England, there came a shout from ahead.

Then came the clash of steel against steel as swords met. The rebels had waited until the army was fully ensconced and relaxed before attacking. Devereaux stood there panic-stricken. He was going to have to fight anyway. Oh gods alive, he could almost feel the daggers in his chest. Well, he could fight or …

With a cry of cowardly terror, Lord Essex turned tail and fled. Behind him he could hear the sound of his army fighting to the death.

* * *

"Your Majesty, I come bearing bad news," said Devereaux, kneeling in front of the Queen. He had stolen a boat and rowed desperately back across the Irish Sea, almost capsizing several times. He had been thinking hard on the way back and had his story all thought out.

Elizabeth frowned. This could be bad. "Carry on, Lord Devereaux."

"Ma'am, the army I led was surrounded and we fought bravely, but we only just managed to get away with our lives. There were only a few of us left and the others were so badly wounded that they died on the way back. I am all that is left of the force."

This sounded all wrong to Queen Bess, but she was still willing to give him the benefit of the doubt—that is until two hours after Devereaux left.

A ragged figure staggered in. It was Devereaux's commander and stepfather, General Robert Dudley, bloodied and almost dead with exhaustion. "Y … Your Majesty," the man croaked and collapsed before her.

Elizabeth was astonished. She quickly called for doctors to help the man and soon he came around.

"Your Majesty, I bring terrible news."

"I know. Lord Devereaux told me that you had all been killed."

Dudley's face grimaced in anger. "Devereaux had nothing to do with it," he growled. "When the first clash of steel came, he turned and ran. Ma'am, he is a damned coward and I don't care if he is Your Majesty's Lord of Essex and my stepson, you will never get me to serve under him again." The man continued to mutter, "Six of us left—that's all—just six. Damn you, Devereaux, I'll disinherit you."

Elizabeth's jaw dropped. So her initial feelings were correct. Here was concrete proof. Her face scowled in anger as she turned slowly to a footman nearby. "Bring Milord Essex before me at once."

* * *

"Your Majesty, please forgive me," cried the young nobleman as he knelt before his sovereign. Devereaux knew that his life could very well be forfeited for cowardice. He trembled as Elizabeth ground her teeth. Finally, after what to him seemed a century and a half, she spoke.

"Milord Essex, I feel I have badly overestimated your prowess on any sort of battlefield. It seems, sir, that you ran away in the face of the enemy. Devereaux, that is cowardice of the worst sort, for you left your men to die while you saved your own miserable skin." The Queen's voice sank to a whisper. "Sir, do you realise that out of your army of over seven hundred men-at-arms, only six survived—six and *their* blood is on *your* hands!"

At a loss for words, Devereaux could only mumble incoherently in terror.

Elizabeth spoke again. "Sir, you are hereby stripped of your titles to your lands. Herald, let it be known throughout England that this man has no duchy in this country now. Devereaux, you may retain your title of duke, but that is all. You may find yourself a home somewhere in England, but never cast a shadow on the castle gate *ever* again!"

Devereaux's jaw dropped. He was destitute. What good was a ducal title if it had no duchy to back it up? Weeping in horror and remorse, he turned and slunk out of the throne room, not even bothering to bow.

The Lord Chamberlain started after him for such a flagrant breach of palace etiquette, but the Queen raised her hand. "No sir, let the man go. He has paid for his crime and he will never be here again."

The great Queen Bess could not have been more wrong.

* * *

The bow-shouldered form of Devereaux, Lord Essex, second to the title, staggered through the slums of London's East End. The streets and people around him were filthy, the houses nothing more than hovels. But obliterating all else was the horror in his mind. He was beggared for his cowardice. All that day he wandered aimlessly, weeping occasionally and finally ended up at a tavern.

As he sat in the noisy atmosphere, consuming a farthing tankard of mead—his third—he turned away two of the bawdy women who frequented the place. Besides, he could not have afforded the eight-pence[6] they asked. His mind sank lower from the effects of the potent honey liquor. As he thought over what happened, his despair slowly turned to anger. The Queen had no right to take away his lands and his duchy. Devereaux ground his teeth. He was a nobleman of England. He would get even—somehow. Curse that confounded woman. He would see her off the throne and himself in

---

[6] Modern Equivalent: £70

total power over all the land ... no, the world.

* * *

Eldred of Redruth had given up tin mining in Cornwall and come to London to seek his fortune. Unfortunately he had fallen in with bad company and become something of a "soldier of fortune." He listened as the young nobleman in front of him poured out his story and he smiled to himself. Here was a sucker if he ever heard one.

"Arll reet, sir," he sniveled in his Cornish accent. "Pay me twenty croons and oi'll give thee a paarty of men who'll help thee with t' plaans."

Devereaux blanched. Twenty crowns was five pounds, the value of a coach-and-four. It was almost all the money he had, but what if his plan came to fruition? That was enough to make up his mind. With the possibilities parading before his mind's eye, Lord Essex paid the money and the ruffian quickly made away.

Devereaux sat in the inn and waited. About two hours later, Eldred was back. "Oi 'ave spread t' word for thee and t' men will be waiting in St James' Park just afore sunrise."

"How many will there be?"

"'Ard to say," said the ruffian, "but there'll be queete a number. Now Oi must goo. Oi have maach to arreenge."

And the man was gone.

* * *

At 5:34 a.m., Devereaux was grinding his teeth as he turned into St James' Park, London Central. Ahead in the darkness, he saw a large mob of what he guessed to be about two hundred and fifty men standing there. Devereaux smiled. At last, here was his rebellion. He could take over the whole kingdom with this bunch.

"My friends." he began, "follow me and you will no longer be down-at-heel, but noblemen in your own right. I will give you lands and riches beyond your wildest dreams. We march now to take what rightfully belongs to us—the Kingdom of Britain itself."

As he turned imperiously, he did not notice the slight sniggering from the back of the mob as they turned to follow their so-called leader.

* * *

The sun was rising as the mob strode down the approach and came to a halt in front of St James' Palace.

"Open in the name of Devereaux, Lord Essex," cried Devereaux, a sword raised.

"Who demands entrance?" shouted the voice of the guard.

"Devereaux, Lord Essex. Surrender or we will sack the palace."

The guard's face appeared over the battlements. "Really?" he sneered. "Thee and whose army?"

Devereaux clenched his teeth in anger. This upstart would be the first against the wall when he, Devereaux, was king. "Mine, you heap of pig droppings. My army and I will stop at nothing to take what is *rightfully* mine."

The guard looked behind him. "I repeat: thee and whose army?"

There was a loaded pause.

Devereaux felt an icy chill slide down his spine as he became aware of a horrible emptiness behind him. He looked around. The men were gone except for some that he saw fleeing in the distant streets. He could hear their derisive laughter. He had given them their five pence, enough to feed themselves and their families for at least four weeks and now they wanted nothing to do with the young nobleman. Eldred himself had made fourteen shillings. He was in the money.

Devereaux felt terribly foolish. His rebellion had ended before it started. Then terror took over along with his natural cowardice. He dropped the sword and took to his heels.

The guard began to laugh as he went off to report to the Queen.

* * *

"He *what?*" cried Elizabeth.

"He stood right in front of the palace gate, Your Majesty, on his own. I believe he thought he had an army behind him when he demanded entrance to sack t' palace."

"And he named himself?"

"Aye, Your Majesty: 'Devereaux, Lord Essex,' that's what 'e said, not once but twice."

"Just a minute. What was his accent?"

"Oh, t'were a nobleman's accent, Your Majesty."

"Oh." The Queen sat there, her brow furrowed. The idea that Devereaux was being framed occurred to her, but why? No reason that she could see. Finally she came to a decision. "I command that Devereaux, Lord Essex, be captured as soon as possible and taken to the tower for beheading," she intoned. "Proclaim it to the far reaches of the kingdom. The hue and cry is to be raised. He will not be responsible for any more uprising. In God's name, I command it."

The guard hurried out as a secretary began swiftly writing the proclamation.

* * *

"Did you hear? Essex is to be captured and beheaded," said Bacon, his wig almost falling off in his excitement. He and Dee had met in the street outside Bacon's abode.

"B ... but why?" asked Dee, shocked.

"He tried to lead a rebellion against the Queen, but then," said Bacon, laughing. "The men he was leading turned and fled and left him in the lurch. He ... . Listen!"

In the near distance, they heard the voice of the town crier. "Oyez! Oyez! Devereaux, Lord Essex is pronounced *persona non grata*. Anyone knowing of his whereabouts is to inform the castle. He is to be brought to the tower and there his head shall be separated from his body. God save the Queen. Oyez! Oyez …"

Bacon went on laughing. "He was left standing alone outside the palace gate, brandishing a sword and demanding entrance so he could sack the castle—and with nothing to back him up. Twice the guard challenged him with 'thee and whose army,' and twice Essex referred to the great army behind him. Then, in response to the guard's challenge, Essex turned to face his presumed army, only to find he stood there alone. It must have been quite a sight."

Dee shook his head and chuckled. "Well so much for Devereaux and to think I once liked the man. I am afraid I shall not want to meet him ever again."

* * *

At that moment Devereaux was on a horse, fleeing London. He had ridden hard for five miles and stopped only to let his horse rest. Terror stalked his heels and Devereaux looked about him, expecting to be leaped on and captured at any minute.

"Now what do I do?" he moaned quietly. He had gone from being a favourite of the Queen to being a fugitive on the run from justice. As if in answer to his plight, he remembered a particular page in Dee's translation of—*what was it called now … .ah yes, The Necronomicon*. Devereaux's face became an evil smile of utter malice as he recalled Dee's careful lettering.

Ye Counjuration of the Opening of ye Door to All Power, Knowledge and Enlightenmente.

The man nodded. Yes, that would do nicely. He turned his horse and, as the sun dipped to the horizon, returned to London. He knew of a secret entry into the city which would give him cover from the guard.

* * *

It was 4:47 a.m. and London was silent—well, not quite.

Nearby at Dee's house, a furtive footstep was muffled by the thick fog as Devereaux, having left his horse in the courtyard, forced open the door silently and crept into the Dee's home, intending to plunder. He made for Dee's workroom.

He entered the room, closed the door and quickly lit a candle. He found the translation just where Dee had left it. Leafing through the pages, he found the page he sought and also the following pages which completed the dreaded spell. Baring his teeth in a ferocious grimace, he bundled them up and pushed them into a pocket. *I'll leave the candle burning,* he thought. *It may burn down the house and keep anyone from finding the rest of the scroll.*

Quickly he leaped onto his horse. It was a mark of the man's selfishness that he didn't stop to think his actions could lead to the death of the doctor and others in the surrounding wooden buildings.

Thankfully, Doctor John Dee was a light sleeper and was awakened by the clattering of horse's hooves. He shook his head to get the sleep out of his eyes. Becoming aware of the human requirement to answer the call of nature, he climbed out of bed. He saw no sign of anything in the darkened street below his bedroom and thought he must have imagined the sound he heard.

He realised a light was burning downstair when he saw it reflected on the wall of the house opposite. Quickly wrapping a robe around him, he hurried downstairs and saw a candle burning in his workroom. Swallowing hard, Dee entered. At first glance, all seemed to be in order. Then he saw it—the translation of *The Necronomicon* was open. He hurried around the desk and looked down at the page and swallowed even harder. He recognised the page open in front of him. It was the spell which followed the big spell—the spell that opened the door. He quickly turned back the pages and horror struck his soul as he realised that the awful spell was gone. Oh, God's wounds. What should he do now?

Dee suddenly felt helpless. A terrible spell was more or less on the loose. Devereaux—Dee was sure it was him—was the only person other than Dee who had seen the scroll and knew its contents. Devereaux would cast the spell and heaven only knew what would happen then.

*　*　*

Deveraux thought he had lost his way in the fog until he suddenly saw the ghostly frame of London Bridge, which led out to the east. He dug in his spurs and rode like the wind.

The guard at London Bridge attempted to challenge the rider but was buffeted to one side as the horse rattled passed. He shook his head as he watched the man ride over the bridge with a clatter and fade away into the foggy darkness. *It makes our presence almost useless*, he thought gloomily.

Devereaux's horse thundered on in the darkness. The road Devereaux followed led southeast through the kingdom of Kent, past Canterbury and thence to Dover. He had the spell and now the world was his. His mind exalted over what he could do with the spell to end all spells.

He stopped the horse under an overlying tree. Quickly he struck his tinderbox to light his lantern, took out the page and began to read. He realized he needed certain items and also had to be on a hilltop, or at least have an open sky overhead. Devereaux looked wryly at the thick forest showing the light of dawn through the branches. There was no open ground anywhere nearby, nor would there be for several hundreds years. Then he looked toward Dover. The cliffs there would be open to the sky.

Quickly remounting, he galloped through Canterbury and some hours later drew near to Dover. As the sun rose, he found the edge of the huge chalk cliffs in front of him and came to a halt, his horse blowing hard. Before him lay the English Channel.

Now was the time. Without a thought, he went to a small village nearby and, unobserved, stole the items he needed from the home of a blacksmith and from an inn. It was almost midday when he got back to the top of the cliff. After a strong draft of ale, he began to set up the evil altar.

* * *

"Open! In the name of God Almighty, open!" The voice that shouted from the street was panic stricken. The shouts were accompanied by a fusillade of hammering on the door as Bacon's butler unlocked and opened it.

Dee almost tumbled into the room. "Sir Francis! Is he here?"

The butler had been trained to let nothing faze him. He answered slowly and unflappably, "Sir, he is at this moment rising. Whom shall I say … ?"

"Doctor John Dee. Now, you oaf—God's wounds—get him here, now!"

"Very good, sir, would you like to wait in the libr—"

"No, dammit! I would not like to wait in the thrice-accursed library. Get your master here at once."

"Very good, sir," replied the butler, his face completely calm and not giving away a scrap of what he was thinking—this particular piece of aristocracy should be hanged and then drawn and quartered with blunt knives. He turned and walked elegantly away from the fuming doctor and mounted the stairs. He had not gone more than three steps when his master's face appeared at the top.

"Marmaduke, who is that shouting?"

Marmaduke was still totally unfazed. "Doctor John Dee, sir, who apparently would like to see you as soon …"

"I know. If he wants to see me, then get him up here. It must be important."

"Very good, sir." The butler turned to the door. "Doctor Dee, sir, Sir Francis would be glad to see you in his bedr—"

He was talking to empty air. Belying his advanced years, Dee had charged past him and up the stairs three at a time.

"Bacon! In God's name, I need some assistance. Devereaux has robbed me."

Bacon stood there aghast. Theft was not unknown, of course, but who would want to rob the old doctor? Indeed, what could anyone possibly want from this man's house?

Dee went on, "You know the scroll that I am translating?"

"Oh yes, Nec-er-nack—something or other."

"*The Necronomicon. It has some very powerful spells in it, one of which looks dangerous. It opens the door to all power and Devereaux has stolen it!*"

The writer looked at the doctor and thought, *All power. Oh no.*

Dee paused and then continued, "I don't know what the spell is capable of, but in the hands of Devereaux it could be the end of life on Earth."

Bacon slowly nodded. He was not a superstitious man, but he did realise that Dee was not lying and the doctor's knowledge of the unknown was not to be trifled with.

"All right, let's try and find out where he went. It will give us something concrete on which to build."

* * *

The London Bridge gate guard had changed not five minutes before and as the two approached the post, a familiar cry rang out, "Halt! Who goes there?"

"Doctor John Dee and Sir Francis Bacon."

"Your purpose?"

"We wish to enquire if any of your guards saw anyone pass around two hours into the middle watch?"

The guard commander was just about to answer in the negative when one of the guardsmen spoke up, "Sir, I took t' middle and at about two hour into it a horse and rider passed at such speed as I was unable to stop 'em, let alone identify 'em."

"Why did you not tell me about this?"

"Sir," replied the guard apologetically, "I have not yet made my report to 'ee."

Bacon nodded. He felt quite relieved. This was the second guard post they had tried. The first was to the west and was without joy.

The commander nodded with a slight grin and turned back to the two. "There you have your story, sir—a horseman passed at great speed at that time. This road leads to Canterbury and thence to the cliffs at Dover."

"Anywhere else?" asked Dee.

"Only a few small villages, northward is a bypass road through Canterbury and southward there is a small road off to Hastings. But almost nobody travels that way now—there being the more lucrative and considerably safer way of travelling southward through Tunbridge."

"Any wide-open places?"

"Wide-open? *Hmmph*. Well, only one, sir. The only place that could be described as such would be the cliffs of Dover."

Bacon nodded. Then he beckoned Dee away. "We must take a man of the cloth with us," he said, "so that if the spell is cast there will be someone to pronounce an avaunting."

Dee nodded. Though he himself was a priest, he realised the need for someone far more experienced in such things than he. "We must go to Canterbury on the way. The cathedral has many priests who will do the job."

So saying, the two rode swiftly east into the English woodlands.

* * *

Tam of Clachintuna (which later became modern Clacton on Sea) and his wife Lydia were walking to pray at Canterbury. It was a pilgrimage Lydia had wanted to make for quite a few years and to his dismay, Tam had been dragged along for the ride. He could ill afford the time, busy as he was with his squire's garden. As they walked, there came from behind the sound of hooves galloping fast. Before they could look around, two horses came around the corner behind them and they were buffeted into the ditch alongside the road.

Knee deep in muddy water, Tam picked himself up and looked around. Lydia was picking herself up, a look of outrage on her face.

"How ... how *dare* they," she began, her voice starting the usual climb to a fishwife shriek. "How ... *dare* ..."

"Lydia, shut up." The man's voice was quiet, but held a strength that Lydia had never heard before.

"What ... ?"

"I said, shut up."

The man looked around and shrugged his shoulders. He had had enough. "Now listen, I said it before and I'll say it again. I never wanted to go to Canterbury. If you wish to continue on this pilgrimage, you are quite welcome, but I am going home. I have enough to do there without going on some ridiculous religious journey which does nobody any good." Matching his actions to his words, he climbed up the small bank onto the road and picked up his bundle where it had fallen. He turned back and started to walk.

"Tam!" came her shout. "Where do you think you're going?"

"I told you. I'm going home."

"But ... but we wanted to go on this pilgrimage."

Tam turned and scowled. "No, my dear, *you* wanted to go on the pilgrimage. I am sick of doing what *you* want to do. I'm going home to take care of my lord's home and garden. You can do what you like," he said and walked on.

Soon, he heard puffing behind him and turning, saw Lydia. For a few moments, nothing was said and then her arm slipped into his. They looked at each other and slowly started to smile.

"I love you, Tam."

"I love you, Lydia."

The two walked on—homeward bound.

* * *

The Dean of Canterbury, an old man who was nobody's fool, listened to the men's story. What they were asking could be extremely dangerous and he stroked his beard thoughtfully.

"Sirs, I shall choose the finest of our priests for this most auspicious of missions," he said and turned to a black-clad figure by the door. "Deacon, summon Father James Hogarth."

The little priest, interrupted in the middle of prayers, hurried in. When he heard the mission, he licked his lips and bowed. "It will be my honour to join you, fellow Christians," he declaimed and quickly gathered a small bag of necessaries before following them out the door.

The dean breathed a heavy sigh of relief. He himself was too terrified to go and sent the first man he could think of.

Taking to horse, the three dashed out of the courtyard as the dean pronounced a blessing.

"Who was that, Dean?" came the archbishop's rich, fruity voice from behind him.

"Nothing for you to worry about, Your Grace," murmured the dean.

* * *

The three men, riding hard, finally came to the cliffs of Dover. The sea lay ahead and the forests around them were thick and practically impenetrable. It was just starting to rain as they came out of the treeline and saw the edge of the cliff.

"Look around," cried Bacon. "He can't have gone far."

The three separated. Dee went south, Bacon went southwest to investigate a track they had passed on the way in and the priest followed a path northwards along the top of the cliffs. He had not gone far when he came around a curve and saw a cliff edge with a large sandstone rock. Upon the rock lay a strange collection of articles and in front of it—hands raised to the sky and chanting a strange, evil-sounding verse—stood Robert Devereaux.

Clasping his crucifix to his chest, Hogarth retraced his steps, his heart beating fast in terror. The little priest had only been a man of the cloth for five years and this was the first time he had ever come close to utter evil. For a man of his stature, it was an overwhelming feeling. He gave a long, low whistle and, in a moment, the other two joined him.

"He's there," muttered Hogarth, pointing back the way he had come. "I saw him. It looks like he has already started the spell."

"Right, we must take action at once," replied Dee and they began to walk slowly and soundlessly toward the evil altar.

* * *

Devereaux read out the last word, but nothing happened. He looked up at the dark and threatening sky expecting at least a thunderclap, but still nothing.

"Having trouble?"

Devereaux spun around, his heart in his mouth and saw a stranger standing there.

"Who are you?" Devereaux's voice cracked in fear.

The figure drew back its hood. Two extremely old eyes gleamed at him from a dark, handsome, swarthy face as the figure replied, "My name is not really important, but since you ask, it is Barrett Muerte. You seem to be having trouble. Maybe I can help?"

Eyebrows raised, Devereaux suddenly realised that this figure was at least a magician or a sorcerer. "Do you have knowledge of the *unknowable*?"

Unfazed by the other's pointed expression, Muerte nodded, a slight enigmatic smile on his face. "I feel I can indeed help."

Devereaux nodded and clenched his lips. "I cannot get this to work."

Muerte looked sideways at him. "All right, let's hear how you say these words. You may very well be mispronouncing them."

Slowly the two went through the spell and suddenly Muerte put his hand on the other's arm. "How did you pronounce that?"

"Fegara," replied the duke.

"No, no, no! It has a gutteral sound, *fekara*," said the other, sounding the *k* deep in his throat.

Devereaux nodded and copied the sound.

Muerte nodded. "That's it."

They continued on and Muerte repronounced three other words for the duke. When they reached the end, Devereaux smiled. The spell was correct and now he could cast it. He turned to thank his mentor, but there was no sign of him. Devereaux looked around. Barrett Muerte had disappeared as if he had never been there, but that was of no consequence. Now he could open the door and be all powerful.

Heart pounding in greedy glee, he started from the beginning of the spell again. This time he got it right. As he talked, he suddenly found the words pouring unbidden from his mouth. Eventually he just read down the page and his mouth pronounced the words clearly without any effort from him. When he reached the bottom of the page, he didn't even have to turn the page for the last four lines. They were already saying themselves in his mouth. With sweat pouring from his body, he finished the evil spell.

* * *

Dee, Bacon and Hogarth came out of the trees just as Deveraux pronounced the final word. They heard an ear-splitting crash and the heavens opened to a deluge of rain as a huge black door almost fifty feet high and half as wide appeared. It backed onto the clifftop and looked as if it would give access to empty air over the edge of the cliff if it were opened. In front of it lay a silver path. The three stopped dead and stared at the so-called door to everyone's deepest dreams—or deadliest nightmares.

Devereaux's eyes were wide with terrible glee when, out of the corner of his eye, he suddenly caught sight of the three standing in the downpour. He leered at them.

"Greetings, slaves!" he shouted above the roar of the rain. "Enjoy the last few moments of your freedom, for as soon as I walk to this door and open it, the whole world will be enslaved to *me*."

Dee found his voice. "Robert, you can't. That door will not open on power for you, but on the minions of hell."

"Hell?" shouted the duke. "You pitiful old man. The only hell it will open on will be your slavery." With a greedy laugh, he stepped onto the silver path.

Dee's mouth opened and shut like a fish as he realised that there was nothing else he could say that would stop Devereaux from opening the Door of Hell. Sweat poured down his face as he stared impotently while Lord Essex stepped boldly through the curtain of rain toward the door … and hellish oblivion.

Bacon looked at Dee and realised just how evil the door was. Up until this moment he had doubted, but now he was certain. He had to stop the evil duke. Taking a deep breath and realising that it could very well be the last thing he did on this Earth, the big man leaped up onto the silver path. The rain ceased as suddenly as it had started. Bacon desperately tried to hurry after the other man who was striding quickly in front of him. Time seemed to slow for Bacon. Devereaux was hurrying on ahead, seeming to outdistance him.

Behind him Bacon could hear footsteps—the quick steps of the priest. Hogarth had his crucifix in his hand, raised high overhead as he followed the big man, fully aware of what he was going to attempt to do.

Dee, his jaw open in dismay, was torn between flight and loyalty as he watched his friend and the priest attempting to stop the unthinkable from happening.

Devereaux was exalting. It was happening. At last he would be ruler of the whole world. He could hear footsteps behind him, but he was too near his goal. The great black door loomed before him.

He opened his mouth and raised his arms.

"Aza..."

The rest of the terrible name was obliterated as Bacon cannoned into Devereaux, knocking him face first against the jet-black door. The big man grabbed the stunned Devereaux by the scruff of the neck and heaved him sideways. The two fell from the path onto the wet grassy bank and rolled over, ending upright on the cliff edge with Bacon sitting astride his nemesis. The wind from the bottom of the cliffs suddenly howled around them and the water from the downpour emptied over the cliff edge, soaking them both even more. Devereaux desperately tried to unseat his captor, but Bacon was just too heavy. If he could have managed it, Devereaux would have launched the big man over his head and over the cliff, to be killed on the rocks far below.

"Sir! Cease and desist from this insanity immediately!" roared Bacon, his wispy hair flying in the wind. His wig had been lost on the headlong rush from London.

Gasping with the weight of the man on his lower chest, Devereaux—his nose oozing blood from the impact against the door—snarled up at him. "Never, sir! How dare you! I have come too far to be forestalled now. You will never stop me and when I am emperor, you ... you ignorant non-entity will be the first on the drawing beam." The evil duke's expression became one of horrible malice. "I shall *personally* take pleasure in hanging and drawing and quartering you."

"You will do naught of the sort!" shouted Bacon.

Devereaux snarled. Then before Bacon could stop him he shouted, "*Azathoth!*"

"Oh God, no!" screamed Dee, holding his head with his hands, terrified sweat rolling down his face.

Hogarth was still standing on the silver path and gaped up at the gigantic door in sheer horror as it suddenly swung wide with a *whoosh*. Instead of seeing air over the channel, which the priest had expected, he saw nothing but stygian darkness. Then came a huge chuckling sound—like a million oversized bats squeaking—accompanied by a cloud of the most disgusting, evil-smelling smoke that issued from the opening. Hogarth reeled back, a hand to his nostrils desperately trying to stop the disgusting smell.

What happened next haunted Dee and Bacon for many nights thereafter. A voice roared in their heads, one which seemed to echo all around.

Quail, mortals, I am Azathoth. The voice became horribly patronising; My dear, dear Devereaux, I don't know what you thought you were doing, but thanks to you I am now free. Freeee. Haaa! You are witnessing the last day of human life on Earth.

Dee's mind went blank in terror. He stood with his mouth open as the unthinkable occurred. A huge tentacle dripping slime shot out and enfolded Father Hogarth as he turned to run. Screaming, the little priest was lifted high overhead, the crucifix waving impotently in the air.

Bacon forgot Devereaux and scrambled to his feet. He stood there stunned as the scene of utter horror acted out in front of him. The tentacle was squeezing tighter and tighter and drawing the little man toward the huge jet-black opening, which was looking more and more like a great gaping mouth. Hogarth was sure there was no hope for him. His horror released itself in a last long shriek of despair.

But Dee now found his mind acting with unusual clarity. The danger around was so real that his mind slowed down his perception of time and he remembered that other spell from the book on closing an evil portal; the one he had memorised. The few brain cells still working coherently suddenly felt glad he remembered. He desperately tried to swallow his fear and concentrate.

He had to imagine an iron band around his head. Right! He could feel it around his brow. Then he imagined holding a fur-bound book. Yes, there it was! His fingers could almost feel the fur.

Desperately he managed to do this in spite of the horror around him. He raised his hand, drew the strange figure in midair and shouted the seven-syllable word in a trembling voice.

The strange syllables seemed to hang in the air as he said them. The effect was dramatic. There came a thunderous roar of frustration from the black entry, almost deafening those around it and the priest felt the horrifying squeeze suddenly release. He yelled in terror as he was dropped. He landed on his back with a damp thump in a patch of deep, wet grass.

A lightning bolt accompanying a crash of thunder, struck the strange tentacle and it retreated in a knee-jerk reaction. Then the door suddenly slammed shut, chopping off the end of the tentacle with a horrible squelching sound. The door, the path and the tentacle seemed to evaporate. All was silent except for the gentle patter of the rain.

The four men could hardly believe the terrifying horror that had just taken place. Then another voice spoke quietly.

"Well done, James, John and Francis. Your faith and industry has saved the world from the evil one."

Bacon and Dee fell to their knees as the voice fell silent. Tears fell from Dee's eyes.

"Oh Lord," he whispered, "I am so sorry. I did not realise. I promise I will deal with that dreadful book as soon as I return to London."

Bacon gaped. "John, that was … that was … the Infinite. Oh God."

Dee nodded and quickly retrieved the loose pages from the altar, folding them loosely and stuffing them into his robe. Then he swept the other accoutrements from the altar and threw them over the side of the cliff where they fell to oblivion. As they did so, the man pronounced an avaunting, effectively cleansing the site.

In the meantime, Devereaux had scrambled to his feet and was standing there, arms wide, knees trembling and sweat pouring down his face. His mouth fell open and his eyes stared in utter horror. "Oh, God's wounds!" he gasped. "I never knew! I never knew!"

Bacon's mind suddenly released its anger and he turned on the traitor, his teeth bared in fury. "Of course you never knew!" he shouted. "How could you? You never even bothered to find out what could be the consequences of your actions, did you? I am sorely tempted to throw you over the cliff so you can join the articles of your evil in the rocks at the bottom."

Devereaux's face turned white and his eyes showed sheer terror.

"But I will not, as I want you to face justice. Sir, I hereby arrest you in the name of Queen Elizabeth. You will accompany me back to the castle—there to be tried by Her Majesty and no doubt beheaded for being the traitor you are."

"Never," Devereaux shouted and wrenching himself free from the big man's grasp, he turned to run.

Unfortunately his luck ran out when a branch met his head with a sickening *thwack* as he turned. He dropped unconscious to the ground.

Dee looked at his friend, mouth open with concern. "I hope I didn't kill him," he said, dropping the dead branch he had picked up.

Bacon grinned wryly. "No sir, you did not. He will answer. See to Father Hogarth."

The priest had a twisted wrist and was quite winded from his fall. He was soaked through, but otherwise unhurt thanks to the grassy landing. After binding the priest's wound and tying up Devereaux, the three mounted their horses to go back to London. Devereaux's horse had been spooked by the thunder and lightning and was gone, so he had nothing to ride.

"What about me?" shouted the duke. "I can't walk all the way back to London. It's almost eighty miles."

"Yes, it is, isn't it?" said Bacon nastily. "And you, sir, are going to walk the full eighty. Come along now, it's a long way."

Bacon started his horse forward with the rope holding Devereaux tied to the saddle horn. Devereaux had no option but to follow or be dragged. Stumbling, panting and crying, the traitor was made to walk the whole eighty miles to the capital.

* * *

Elizabeth looked at the man lying prostrate and footsore before her, covered in trail dust and mud. The man who had attempted to overthrow her and open the gates to hell smelled and was almost dead from exhaustion. He had been pelted with rotten fruit and vegetables, to say nothing of the contents of numerous night vases, by the populous as Bacon's horse dragged him through the streets to the castle.

Bacon had made representation and described honestly all that occurred. As he did so, the courtiers round about paled and several of them looked physically sick. Now he stood to one side to see what would eventuate.

The Queen had never been so angry. "Devereaux, you … you Judas!" she yelled in fury. "There is nothing left for you on this Earth. You will now be taken to the tower and there your head shall be separated from your body. May God have mercy on your soul, because I—certainly—will—not."

Deveraux—tearful and screaming—was dragged—limping, panting, ordure and dust-covered—from the throne room.

The Queen turned to Bacon. "Where is Dee? I want to congratulate him."

"Your Majesty, I think he feels he has caused enough pain and has returned home. I don't know what he intends to do, but I think it might entail that scroll he was translating."

Queen Bess nodded. "I see. Well, we must see that he receives a goodly pension for his efforts." She looked at Bacon with a wide smile. "You sir, for your prowess, boldness and bravery will receive one hundred golden sovereigns and your lands and holdings will be increased tenfold. We thank you for literally saving the Earth."

Speechless, Bacon bowed.

The Queen then turned to the little priest alongside him. "Father James," she said smiling, showing a trace of tears. "My dear priest, you were willing to sacrifice your own soul for the good of the nation and the Earth. You shall return to Canterbury with an equal amount of gold to do with as you see fit and we thank you most sincerely." She rose and took a sword from the display on the wall nearby. "Kneel, my good priest."

The Victoria and George Crosses were far in the future, of course, but Elizabeth did what she could. Gently she touched the priest on both shoulders.

"I knight thee, Father James Hogarth, for bravery under the most dangerous circumstances, for your outstanding valour in the face of unutterable evil and for services to church, Queen, country—and indeed planet. Arise, Sir James Hogarth, Knight of the Queen's Gratitude."

Totally overcome, the little priest could only nod and smile, tears rolling unashamedly down his cheeks, as he rose from his genuflect. Bacon, a knight already, embraced the man, enjoying the other's emotions.

James Hogarth was utterly overjoyed. Two days later he returned to Canterbury rejoicing. In later years, he became Most Reverend Sir James Hogarth, Archbishop of Canterbury, KQG.

* * *

Doctor John Dee sat at his workroom table in his house in the West End of London. In front of him lay *The Necronomicon* and the translation. *I will finish it*, he thought. *It seems such a shame to waste it, evil though it is.*

He rewrote the great spell quickly from the crumpled paper that Devereaux had stolen and inserted it in the correct place. Then, with his heart in his mouth, he rolled to the last page of the parchment scroll that contained the line of ink that told of a terrified exit. Dee sadly shook his head and, took a deep breath before translating the last page.

Two days later Dee was announced into the throne room. Stepping forward to face the throne, the elderly doctor placed the finished product, now appropriately bound into book form, on the floor before the Queen.

"Ma'am, with the greatest respect, I present to you the final copy of *Al Azif: The Necronomicon*. It has cost more than any will know in blood and toil, as well as great danger, but then you already know that."

The Queen smiled broadly. "Well done, my good doctor. You will receive holdings appropriate to your bravery. Now, what of the original?"

"Sealed in a packet, Ma'am, with stone weights attached. I was thinking of dropping it into the English Channel."

The Queen nodded. "A good idea, make it so."

* * *

"Be this a good place, Zurr?" rolled the deep voice of the boatman with the Summerset accent, as he dropped sail and brought the boat to a standstill halfway across an almost still English Channel. The fishing boat rocked lightly with the slight swell.

Dee looked to both sides. There was the coast of Britain and, just as far away, the coast of France. "Yes," he replied, "this will be ideal, my good man. Thank you for your work."

He stood and tossed a large thick parcel overboard. It landed with a splash and the four stone weights Dee had lodged inside dragged it down into the depths of the sea. Dee watched it sink into the inky depths with mixed emotions. On one hand, he was sorry to lose such a valuable book, but on the other, he was pleased to be rid of it.

Finally, it seemed that the evil scroll, *Al Azif* the original

Necronomicon of Abdul Al-Hazred, was placed far beyond mankind's ability to salvage it. Raising his head, the doctor breathed a prayer of thankfulness to the sky. Then he nodded to the boatman to set sail … this time for home.

Neither noticed a large seabird with strange markings take a fast dive from high overhead. With nary a ripple, it disappeared into the water at the same spot where the scroll had been thrown.

* * *

The Queen's librarian, Captain Laurence of Dartmouth, received the translation and carefully sealed it. It was placed in the vault far underground at Windsor Castle. As he did so, he idly read the footnote that Dee had placed on it:

*A warninge to all ye who may wishe to caste the magick within this book. The danger can **notte** be underestimated. 'Tis awfulle in the extreeme. Should thou wishe to attempte a spelle, understande that any consequences shall be upon thy heade.*
Signed,
John Dee (DD)

Laurence smiled wryly. He was not about to cast any spell. He placed it carefully in with the many other books in the safe, closed and locked it. Then he walked away.

The book was left in darkness—for what seemed forever.

* * *

The dungeon door clanged open and a burly guard entered followed by a hooded priest. They stopped opposite a bedraggled figure seated on a stinking rushbed against the wall. The guard bowed and Father John's voice intoned, "M'Lord Essex, thou'rt to be taken this day. Be thee ready?"

Devereaux's face turned pale with terror. He did not move; did not even look up. He sat on the rushes, his lower jaw trembling, his eyes staring into the far distance.

After waiting the required ten seconds, the guard stepped up and hauled Devereaux to his feet. "Cooom on, M'Lord. Thou'rt az ready az thou'll ever be," said the guard and literally dragged him out the door, as the priest followed them intoning the prayers for an executed man. The Latin phrases seemed to swirl around the duke's terror-fogged brain as he was dragged through the dark, filthy dungeon corridors and outside into the large execution square, where a crowd was gathered to greet the duke with shouts of derision.

Also in the square was the executioner, who was standing beside the block, the traditional black mask covering his head. He rested his arms on the top of the long handle of a big double-bladed axe that was held in place between his feet.

After one terrified glance at him, Devereaux's eyes came to rest in horrified fascination on the block in the centre of the square. A detached part of his mind noted the indentation made for the chin and the curve on the opposite side where his shoulders would rest. Then he looked at the basket of straw where his severed head would come to rest and the bloodstains on the cobblestones.

Devereaux looked around desperately, then with a cry of unutterable fear turned to flee, but a strong hand landed on his shoulder, halting him almost where he stood. Mocking laughter came from the crowd as the guard flung the duke onto his knees with a practiced gesture, the duke's head and shoulders coming to rest on the block with a bone-jarring thud. His eyes could see nothing but the straw in the bottom of the basket. Some small detached part of his mind noted that some of it was rotted and had mold on it. The cloying smell filled his nostrils.

Devereaux's terrified little mew was lost in the rolling Latin as the priest brought the swift service to an end.

" ... *Et in NomineParemetFilliietSpiritusSancti. Amen.*"

Father John ran the final words of the Nomine together, crossed himself perfunctorily, then made the sign of the cross in the air over the condemned Duke before closing his book with a slap. Most of the crowd also crossed themselves.

"Now, oh sinner," the priest droned on mechanically, "submit thy soul to God, for 'tis he who will judge thee at the last. Farewell." Wanting to get the prayers over and done with—a bottle of Madeira waited for him back in the vestry—he nodded to the axeman.

The crowd roar had built up until they were all shouting the chant, "Trai—tor. Trai—tor. Trai—tor."

Devereaux felt his shoulders being held down by the guardsman as his chin rested in the indentation. His mind went blank as his cowardice took over. He was about to die. *Oh gods of all, this cannot be happening*, he thought in sheer terror, but just as the axeman brought up his axe, Devereaux heard a chuckle.

The executioner was widely known to be Thomas Derrick, but Devereaux knew that was certainly not Derrick's voice. The duke felt his blood freeze when he recognized the voice.

"Muerte," he gasped.

The axeman paused, his blade poised over his head and time froze. All sound stopped as if cut off with a knife. Even the crowd stood frozen in place.

The duke could hear nothing.

Then came Muerte's mysterious voice, seeming from the mouth of the axeman:

> "Yes, Milord of Essex," sneered Muerte, "and now you will get your just desserts. You cast the spell … and it failed … and now let this be the beginning of your own horror, for now you will answer for it." The man's voice became musing. "You know, even if you had succeeded you would still have been condemned. This was the terrible truth discovered by the original author of the parchment you attempted to exercise, Abdul Al-Hazred. Even

he did not grasp the true nature of the evil he had himself writ till he was writing the last page.

"That page was never finished, such was his mortal terror, which then cost him his sanity, his life and his soul; as our other friends, the delightful Morgan le Fay, wonderfully decadent Reynald De Chatillon and humbly benighted inquisitor general also discovered, to their unbelieving consternation and chagrin. All of them called the name and opened the door. There were those who endeavored to stop them and thereby save the world from the resultant chaos. Well, to that extent, they succeeded. As for the inquisitor general, his disgustingly obscene body was cleaved in twain by an almost casual flick of a hellish claw and all four condemned souls were then sucked through the door to begin their eternal torment.

"That same fate befalls every poor selfish fool who attempts to cast that terrible spell, or any of its cousins, in their sad and pathetic belief that they shall have total power over the world. How the minions of hell laugh as each poor fool opens The Great Door and realizes that instead of achieving absolute power, they are naught but sacrificed pawns. Thus your actions, Milord of Essex, just go to show how totally useless your miserable excuse for a life has been. And now, just before I bid you goodbye, let me also enlighten you.

"For my sins, I was accursed with everlasting physical life. I am countless hundreds of years old. My true name is not Barrett Muerte, but Nyarlathotep and Azathoth is my father. But I have had many names over the millennia. At one point I was known as Nephren-Ka, a priest of ancient Egypt. I am the guardian of the book and it is my task to encourage such pathetically deluded souls as yourself, to discover and utilize one of the spells in this terrible book, so that the great door may be opened when the name of my father, Azathoth, the Crawling Chaos, is called so he may emerge and reign over the world forever. As a matter of fact, there are no less than fifteen spells in that book which, although worded differently, can do exactly the same thing. I thought it best to have a few more strings in my bow. I cannot cast any of the spells myself; such is my curse.

"I am thus accursed to this task for all time. Before the advent of the book, it was very hard to get a wizard to cast a spell using my own devises and I had to use all my guile and willfulness to encourage it. Although I failed, I still managed to condemn no less than fifteen men and women of power. But now my task is so much easier. I still do not know if I will ever achieve this task. I am granted no rest until the task is achieved and much of my endless lifetime is spent waiting. So I utilize the ultimate temptation, offering such deluded souls as you the prospect of absolute power over the world. It never ceases to amaze me that the offer is always accepted so readily, such is the frailty of the human condition and the unutterable greed of mankind.

"Your frailty and greed have brought you to this moment, Milord of Essex. I don't have much to enjoy throughout the eons, but at least I do get to take over the executioner's body for a few moments and execute such as you. Ha! Being an executioner is not all that bad. Milord Duke, when his axe falls you will have all of eternity to reflect upon the futility of your cupidity … as your soul writhes in the agony of eternal despair. Farewell."

Then came the evil chuckle again and the crowd's roar rolled over his head. Time stopped for a moment and began again when the axe fell in an arc perfectly suited to punish his treason to Almighty God, the reigning sovereign, the nation and humanity itself. Devereaux had enough time to think, like a schoolboy, *This is not fair. . .* before his life ended. His head rolled onto the straw in the basket in front of him, blood and gore squirting in all directions.

The priest, executioner and guard heard nothing and what seemed to Devereaux to take two minutes or more passed in an eye blink for the three men.

Thomas Derrick, the executioner, shook his head. For a moment or so, it felt as though someone else was sitting behind his eyes, but he scoffed at this. *What rubbish*, he thought. He received his two-shilling payment, put all other thoughts out of his mind and joined Father John for a Madera.

The remains of Robert Devereaux, Duke of Essex and second of that title, were buried in a potter's field outside the city gates; he was not mourned and only remembered by listings in histories and family trees. There remained a widespread rumour, however, that on cold, dark, stormy nights—of which there are plenty in London—if anyone goes near the unmarked resting place of the cowardly Robert Devereaux and listens carefully, the blood-curdling sound of a soul screaming can be heard—a soul in total everlasting torment that has sold itself to evil and will pay for it—*forever.*

Chapter Seven

AD 1846
Arkham, Massachusetts, United States of America

"What do you want?" asked the head teacher, Eldred Mortimer, of the tiny Salem Academy—soon to be known as Miskatonic University—near the rather strange little town of Arkham.

"Sir," replied the handsome swarthy Middle Eastern man, bowing in almost theatrical solemnity, "I understand your school is interested in things metaphysical and with this in mind, I have a scroll you may find interesting, if not useful." He held out a strange parchment scroll bound with three leather thongs.

"Oh, really?" Mortimer sneered, taking the filthy scroll and carefully unrolling the ancient parchment. He couldn't fail to notice the pronounced water stains at the top and bottom of the pages. However, the old Arabic script was not smudged and the writing was still quite clear. It must be very old to withstand a wetting like that. He went on, "What would I need with such a scroll as this?"

"Oh, you will indeed find it very interesting," replied the man wryly. "It is known as *The Necronomicon*." The horrific name rolled off the man's tongue.

There was a loaded pause. Then Mortimer looked at the title at the top of the first page. "*Hmm. Demon Song*. I see." His expression changed to one of extreme interest. "And your name, sir?"

"Muerte. Barrett Muerte."

* * *

In the deepest vault of the Royal Library in Windsor Castle—unknown to the British Royal Family for almost three centuries—lies the copy of the book in Elizabethan English and in a niche in an unknown cave at the bottom of a deep ravine way outside Madrid lies another copy in Medieval Latin.

Three copies now exist of the dreadful book—one in Britain, one in Spain and the original in America—a book containing such evil that even the wickedest sorcerers, wizards and witches of modern times would not think of casting the spells found within it.

But somewhere there is the undying figure of Nyarlathotep, the dreaded guardian of the book, who will stop at nothing to make sure that the spells are said. All he needs is just one person, one foolish person, to try to cast them. No doubt someday and somewhere, he will find someone wicked enough, foolish enough, or ignorant enough to want to resurrect and use the terrible, evil, deadly spells of... The Necronomicon.

* * *

The place of the Scaffold in London, where Robert Devereaux was executed in 1601, actually exists. Yes, it does, but who was the executioner, Thomas Derrick ... *or someone else?*

Epilogue

Just outside Madrid sometime in the Future

Manuel Gonzales, Corporal of the Spanish Army, had lost the rest of his unit in a huge explosion three days before and had somehow been spared.

Now he was stumbling aimlessly through the blasted back country nursing a wounded leg. His friends were all dead. He had nowhere to go. Instead of lovely fields of grass and crops or herds and vineyards full of Spanish wine grapes, he saw only a terrible wilderness, littered with the burnt remains of great tanks, crashed warplanes, mangled armaments of all types and—most horrible—men's dead bodies. No life existed anywhere at all. The overpowering smell of death was everywhere.

World War III was at long last at an end. Gonzales's head was reeling with the horrors of what he had seen and done. World War I had lasted four years and World War II six. World War III had taken almost fifteen years, completely draining the world's resources. No one could say there was a winner; everyone was a loser. He had no idea if there was anyone left in the cities. The nations of the world had bankrupted themselves by arming their troops to the teeth and the armies were utterly insane: going on senseless rampages throughout the countries and killing friend and foe alike. Some years back, they eventually fought to a standstill and then just murdered each other until they were down to single men.

Those men, unable to live with the knowledge of having killed so many, committed suicide.

Gonzalez shook his head in dismay and utter despair. He had nobody to report to, no plans to make, no maps to study, no orders to obey and indeed no ammunition left to fire. His rifle hung unused from his shoulder. All he wanted was to go home to his mother, his wife, his son and twin daughters, but he knew his home would be in ruins just like the rest of the country and the rest of the world. He shuddered to think about it, but they were probably dead. He only hoped that if they were, it had been quick. The world he had known no longer existed and all thanks to this bloody, horrible, everlasting war.

The man came to a deep ravine—casting doubtful eyes at the huge thunderheads gathering in the sky and becoming aware of the heat from the air about him. Looking down into the fissure, he spied a small cave and thanked God for the shelter.

Following an ancient sheep trail down into the ravine, he took cover just as the sun set and the huge, almost savage downpour began. He quickly took off his march-weary boots and fell into the sleep of the utterly exhausted. Not even the storm thundering its fury overhead could wake him although several horrific nightmares made him roll over a number of times.

The following morning he awoke exactly at six, as he always did, when he thought he heard his sergeant yell, "Up guards and at 'em," as usual, but when he opened his eyes, there was just the morning sun gently lighting the cave … and he was alone.

His stomach growled. *Right, let's see if we can find some breakfast*, he thought without much hope. He had passed the remains of a garden the previous day, which might have something edible in it. Okay, raw vegetables would not make a very good breakfast, but they were better than a rumbling tum. Taking a deep breath, he stood and stretched his cramped muscles. He pulled on his boots, picked up his rifle and was about to exit when his eye fell on something in the niche nearby—a strange old book, roughly bound and looking in rather poor shape.

He picked it up and carefully opened it. It was in Latin. Gonzalez had learned Latin as a schoolboy and had been pretty good at it.

Hmm. Let's see what it says. Uh … Ecce liber terra nigram, Liber Necro Nomica est. The Book of the Black Earth, The Book of Dead Names …

* * *

Two days later, World War IV broke out.

Review Requested:
If you loved this book, would you please provide a review at Amazon.com?

Made in the USA
Monee, IL
03 May 2026

49437706R00080